A BASIC GUIDE TO

Cycling

An Official U.S. Olympic Committee Sports Series

The U.S. Olympic Committee

Griffin Publishing Group

This Hardcover Edition Distributed By
Gareth Stevens Publishing
A World Almanac Education Group Company

This hardcover edition distributed by
Gareth Stevens Publishing
A World Almanac Education Group Company
330 West Olive Street, Suite 100
Milwaukee, WI 53212 USA

For a free color catalog describing Gareth Stevens' list of high-quality books and multimedia programs, call 1-800-542-2595 (USA) or 1-800-461-9120 (Canada). Gareth Stevens Publishing's Fax: (414) 332-3567.
Visit Gareth Stevens' website at: www.garethstevens.com

Library of Congress Cataloging-in-Publication Data for this hardcover edition available upon request from Gareth Stevens Publishing. Fax: (414) 336-0157 for the attention of the Publishing Records Department.

Hardcover edition: ISBN 0-8368-2795-3

Editorial Statement
In the interest of brevity, the Editors have chosen to use the standard English form of address. Please be advised that this usage is not meant to suggest a restriction to, nor an endorsement of, any individual or group of individuals, either by age, gender, or athletic ability. The Editors certainly acknowledge that boys and girls, men and women, of every age and physical condition are actively involved in sports, and we encourage everyone to enjoy the sports of his or her choice.

1 2 3 4 5 6 7 8 9 05 04 03 02 01
Printed in the United States of America

ACKNOWLEDGMENTS

PUBLISHER — Griffin Publishing Group
DIR. / OPERATIONS — Robin L. Howland
PROJECT MANAGER — Bryan K. Howland
WRITER — Suzanne Ledeboer
BOOK DESIGN — m2design group

USOC
CHAIRMAN/PRESIDENT — William J. Hybl

USA CYCLING
EXECUTIVE DIRECTOR — Lisa Voight
CHIEF OPERATING OFFICER — Phil Milburn

EDITORS — Geoffrey M. Horn
Catherine Gardner

CONTRIBUTING EDITORS — USA Cycling
United States Cycling Federation (USCF)
U.S. Professional Racing Association (USPRO)
National Off-Road Bicycle Association (NORBA)

PHOTOS — USOC
USA Cycling
Tandem Club of America
New England Cycling Support Association
Sandra Applegate

COVER DESIGN — m2design group
COVER PHOTO — USOC

Special thanks to USA Cycling for the use of biography information and athlete photos.

The United States Olympic Committee

The U.S. Olympic Committee (USOC) is the custodian of the U.S. Olympic Movement and is dedicated to providing opportunities for American athletes of all ages.

The USOC, a streamlined organization of member organizations, is the moving force for support of sports in the United States that are on the program of the Olympic and/or Pan American Games, or those wishing to be included.

The USOC has been recognized by the International Olympic Committee since 1894 as the sole agency in the United States whose mission involves training, entering, and underwriting the full expenses for the United States teams in the Olympic and Pan American Games. The USOC also supports the bid of U.S. cities to host the winter and summer Olympic Games, or the winter and summer Pan American Games, and after reviewing all the candidates, votes on and may endorse one city per event as the U.S. bid city. The USOC also approves the U.S. trial sites for the Olympic and Pan American Games team selections.

WELCOME TO THE OLYMPIC SPORTS SERIES

We feel this unique series will encourage parents, athletes of all ages, and novices who are thinking about a sport for the first time to get involved with the challenging and rewarding world of Olympic sports.

This series of Olympic sport books covers both summer and winter sports, features Olympic history and basic sports fundamentals, and encourages family involvement. Each book includes information on how to get started in a particular sport, including equipment and clothing; rules of the game; health and fitness; basic first aid; and guidelines for spectators. Of special interest is the information on opportunities for senior citizens, volunteers, and physically challenged athletes. In addition, each book is enhanced by photographs and illustrations and a complete, easy-to-understand glossary.

Because this family-oriented series neither assumes nor requires prior knowledge of a particular sport, it can be enjoyed by all age groups. Regardless of anyone's level of sports knowledge, playing experience, or athletic ability, this official U.S. Olympic Committee Sports Series will encourage understanding and participation in sports and fitness.

The purchase of these books will assist the U.S. Olympic Team. This series supports the Olympic mission and serves importantly to enhance participation in the Olympic and Pan American Games.

United States Olympic Committee

Contents

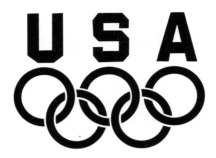

AN ATHLETE'S CREED

The most important thing in the Olympic Games is not to win but to take part, just as the most important thing in life is not the triumph but the struggle. The essential thing is not to have conquered but to have fought well.

These famous words, commonly referred to as the Olympic Creed, were once spoken by Baron Pierre de Coubertin, founder of the modern Olympic Games. Whatever their origins, they aptly describe the theme behind each and every Olympic competition.

Metric Equivalents

Wherever possible, measurements given are those specified by the Olympic rules. Other measurements are given in metric or standard U.S. units, as appropriate. For purposes of comparison, the following rough equivalents may be used.

1 kilometer (km)	= 0.62 mile (mi)	1 mi = 1.61 km
1 meter (m)	= 3.28 feet (ft)	1 ft = 0.305 m
	= 1.09 yards (yd)	1 yd = 0.91 m
1 centimeter (cm)	= 0.39 inch (in)	1 in = 2.54 cm
	= 0.1 hand	1 hand (4 in) = 10.2 cm
1 kilogram (kg)	= 2.2 pounds (lb)	1 lb = 0.45 kg
1 milliliter (ml)	= 0.03 fluid ounce (fl oz)	1 fl oz = 29.573 ml
1 liter	= 0.26 gallons (gal)	1 gal = 3.785 liters

1

Cycling in the Olympic Games

Today, cycling is one of the most technically advanced sports in Olympic competition. Bicycle design and construction are constantly subjected to technological improvements, which are apparent with each passing year. No modern cyclist, nor cycling fan for that matter, would consider the lumbering machines of the 1900 Paris Games as adequate for competitive cycling. Yet cycling owes a great deal to those brave pioneers of the sport who started cycling on its way to becoming an international sport of champions.

Cycling struggled through a difficult growth period before reaching the Olympic superstar status it enjoys today. At the Paris Olympic Games in 1900, there was only one cycling event. Little was recorded about that event, suggesting—perhaps surprisingly, in view of its popularity at the turn of the century—that cycling was not considered a primary Olympic sport.

The situation looked a little brighter for the St. Louis Games in 1904, when seven track races were included in the program as exhibition events; but no nations other than the United States participated in the cycling events. As if that weren't bad enough, fewer than a handful of spectators showed up to watch them.

It appeared that the London Games in 1908 would be a step forward in terms of organization and participation. Track events were scheduled to be held on a banked 500-meter oval inside the main Olympic stadium, thereby allowing an increased number of spectators to attend the cycling competition. Moreover, organizers thought that holding cycling inside the main stadium, where newspaper reporters could be seated comfortably, would practically guarantee expanded, more favorable press coverage. Unfortunately, by the time of the competition, the weather had turned very bad, and spectators stayed away in droves. The competition was held on schedule, but the track surface was wet and slippery, causing many cyclists to slip, slide, and crash. This did not improve the already skeptical media impression of cycling as an Olympic sport, and there was even talk of dropping cycling from future Olympic programs. Fortunately, cooler heads prevailed, and cycling has seen steady growth and support in every Olympics since the wet and slippery Games of 1908.

At present, Olympic cycling consists of three separate categories of racing: track, road, and mountain biking. Track races are held on steeply banked tracks called *velodromes*. Road racing is exactly what the name implies—racing on paved roadways. Mountain bike racing made its debut at the 1996 Olympic Games in Atlanta, bringing a third dimension to cycling: off-road racing.

Track bikes have no brakes and only one gear, which is adjusted according to the riding style of the cyclist and the size of the track. Road bikes are built with sophisticated aerodynamic shifting and braking qualities, and some have as many as 16 gears. Mountain bikes vary, but in general have flatter tires for better off-road traction.

Spectator's Guide

The following spectator guidelines certainly apply to Olympic racing strategies and techniques, but also may be relevant for

Photo courtesy of USOC

Olympic track racing is held on steeply banked velodromes.

other top-caliber events, such as the Tour de France, Pan American Games, and world cycling championships.

At the world championships, professionals and amateurs compete separately for the road race title, while at the national championships professionals and amateurs compete against one another for one title. In 1996, professionals were allowed to compete in cycling in the Olympic Games.

If you are fortunate enough to attend a cycling competition, remember to stay well off the path and allow all riders plenty of room. This is especially important in off-road (or mountain bike) racing, where path boundaries may be harder to define. Cyclists love to have spectators cheer them on, but not if they get in the way.

Road Races

Road races are mass-start events that take place on paved roads. They can be point-to-point races over several days or long loops of 5 to 25 miles in length. Endurance is the main factor in road racing; distances of 100 miles and more for men and 50 miles for women are not uncommon. Moreover, the topography (geographic features of an area or district) may vary from hilly to flat, then hilly again. Each of these features appeals to a particular type of cyclist. For example, lean, lightweight climbers usually prefer racing over the hilly portions of a course, but heavier, more powerful cyclists usually excel on the flat portions of a course. Endurance specialists often force the pace at the front of the pack, while other cyclists deliberately trail, waiting and watching for the opportune moment to burst forward and place themselves in the most advantageous position.

Watch for strong, aggressive riders to *attack* the group in an attempt to *break away* and head out on their own. Because a group can ride faster and with less effort than a soloist can, savvy riders know when—and when not—to employ the individual breakaway technique. If a lone rider runs into strong headwinds or crosswinds, or encounters a difficult hill, the "advantage" of being out front all alone will quickly become a major liability.

Photo courtesy of USOC

Road races are mass events that take place on paved roads.

Another type of breakaway you may see is the *cluster* break in which a number of riders surge forward, forming their own *paceline*. A cluster of riders has a better chance of success, particularly if the cluster contains several riders from a single team. The tip-off is to watch for riders wearing the same jersey. These riders will take turns setting the pace and resting in the draft. Riders from other teams may try to "sit in," refusing to take a turn at the front, or take a shorter turn than the others. The strategy is to try and slow the break, hoping one's own teammates can catch up. Alternatively, a "maverick" rider may employ this technique to move close to the front while conserving energy for a final burst of speed to the finish line.

Watch the front of the main pack. If its leaders wear the same jersey as the breakaway riders, they are *blocking*, trying to keep the pack from chasing the breakaway group. If the leaders of the main pack are wearing jerseys different from those in the group break, a full-scale chase may be developing. Under these conditions, you may well see many lead changes before anyone crosses the finish line. Keep an eye out for the *sprinters*—this is when they make their move to the front.

Track Races

Racing in the velodromes requires a special bike and some equally special skills. Velodromes are not all the same. Some have very gentle banking; others are very steep. Some are elongated with sharp turns, while others are almost round with short straightaways.

All have lines painted on the track's surface. The blue line on the inside of the track marks the track's inner boundary. The sprinter's lane lies between this blue line and a thin red line, higher up on the track. A rider within this area is said to "own the lane," and may only be passed by a competitor who goes up and over. The uppermost thin blue line, called the stayer's line, marks the boundary between faster and slower traffic, with the faster riders below and slower riders above.

Photo courtesy of USOC

Track racing bikes, such as the one ridden here by U.S. Olympian
Rebecca Twigg, have no brakes!

Olympic Track Events

Match Sprints

The match sprint event covers a distance of 1,000 meters,
although timing does not begin until one or more of the riders
crosses the 200-meter mark before the finish line. Typically, two
riders compete against each other in each heat. Usually, riders
perform "flying 200s" individually at the beginning of
competition to determine who will sprint against whom. Match
sprint events typically are games of "cat and mouse," where riders
attempt to outwit each other for the best position during the
first two laps. In addition to outstanding speed and power, the
element of surprise and excellent bike-handling skills are
characteristics of match sprinters.

Points Race

The points race is the longest of all the Olympic track events, usually exceeding 40 kilometers. Riders "sprint" for points every five laps, and usually the top four riders who cross the start/finish line first receive points. Point sprints in the middle of the race and on the last lap are worth double points. One way to win the points race, obviously, is to accumulate the most points, but another way is to "lap" the field. Riders who lap the field are scored ahead of riders with points. Characteristics of successful points racers include good sprinting ability, outstanding endurance, and excellent tactical skills.

Time Trials

Time trials are races against the clock. The rider with the fastest time is the winner. The kilometer time trial and the individual pursuit are individual events, whereas the team pursuit is a team event.

Kilometer

The kilometer time trial is 1,000 meters long, and riders start from a standstill. Because riders are forced to perform at a maximum effort for more than one minute, many people believe this event is one of the most challenging and stressful in track racing. Characteristics of successful kilometer riders include strength, power, and the ability to withstand high levels of stress.

Individual Pursuit

The individual pursuit is a longer time-trial event, with men covering distances of 4,000 meters and women covering distances of 3,000 meters. Riders start pursuit from a standstill, and two riders usually compete at the same time, starting on opposite sides of the track. Some events are structured so that riders qualify on time, even if they do not "catch" the opposing rider. At other events, a rider wins by "catching" the opposing rider. Characteristics of successful pursuit riders include outstanding endurance and excellent pacing ability.

Team Pursuit

In the team pursuit, teams of four riders compete as units against other teams for the best time. In addition, the clock does not stop until the third rider crosses the start/finish line. Teams must work together so that weaker riders are not dropped. In addition to endurance and pacing ability, team pursuit riders must have the ability to work together as a unit. In all other respects, the team pursuit is identical to the individual pursuit.

Off-Road Races

In the United States, the National Off-Road Bicycle Association (NORBA), a division of the USA Cycling, is the governing body for the sport of mountain bike racing. NORBA sanctions racing and touring events throughout the 50 states, and promotes the sport internationally. Cycling made its Olympic debut at the Atlanta Games in 1996. Mountain biking is one of the fastest-growing cycling disciplines. NORBA now has more than 30,000 active members.

At the international level, mountain bike racing was first accepted by the *Fédération International Amateur de Cyclisme* (FIAC)— the world governing body of cycling—in 1990. Its popularity has grown so large that mountain biking now has two world championship events: downhill and cross-country. The downhill is a time-trial event designed to reward the fastest downhill bike racer—on a rather steep hill. A downhill specialist has to be daring and a superb bike handler. For spectators, this is an exciting event, since the action is fast and the rules are straightforward. The scoring is direct and uncomplicated, and the entire event takes place within viewing range.

The basic form of mountain bike racing is the cross-country event; at the 2000 Olympics, the men's course was between 40 and 50 kilometers long, and the women's race was 30-40 kilometers. Riders face a variety of natural hazards, such as sandy slopes, grassy knolls, steep mountains, streams and rivers, and bogs and marshes. Mountain bikers tackle whatever crosses their path. It's hard to see the entire course, but spectators usually like to stand near a stream or hill where different riders make different decisions about how to traverse that hazard. As a result, spectators get to see a greater variety of off-road techniques.

Race times vary according to ability. Beginners usually can finish their course in one hour or less, while the longer pro races may take up to three hours or more.

There are two fundamental rules for mountain bike racing. First, bikes must have wheels no larger than 26 inches, with tires no thinner than 1.5 inches; plugged handlebars; and two independent brakes. Second, each rider must be self-sufficient— no outside assistance or technical support is allowed. (Contrast this with road racers, who usually have elaborate support staffs accompanying them.) The idea behind off-road racing is that every competitor should (and does) have the same chance. The rider who can afford to buy umpteen bikes has no advantage over the rider who has only one bike. In off-road racing, participants finish the race on the bike they began with; substitutions are not allowed. If your bike becomes damaged beyond your ability to make immediate repairs, better luck next weekend. All competitors carry spare inner tubes and tire patches and change all flats themselves, but the winner ultimately is the one who is best able to keep his or her bike out of serious trouble.

U.S. Olympic Cycling Medal Highlights, 1912-1996

1912 Stockholm, Sweden
Individual Road Race (Men)
Carl Schutte   Bronze

1984 Los Angeles, USA
Individual Pursuit (Men)
Steve Hegg   Gold
Leonard Nitz   Bronze

Individual Road Race (Men)
Alexi Grewal   Gold

Individual Road Race (Women)
Connie Carpenter-Phinney   Gold
Rebecca Twigg   Silver

Team Pursuit (Men)
Dave Grylls, S. Hegg, Pat McDonough, L. Nitz   Silver

Match Sprint (Men)
Mark Gorski   Gold
Nelson Vails   Silver

Team Time Trial (Men)
Ron Kiefel, Roy Knickmann,
Davis Phinney, Andy Weaver   Bronze

1988 Seoul, Korea
Match Sprint (Women)
Connie Paraskevin-Young   Bronze

1992 Barcelona, Spain
Individual Pursuit (Women)
Rebecca Twigg   Bronze

1,000-Meter Time Trial (Men)
Erin Hartwell   Bronze

1996 Atlanta, USA
Cross-Country Mountain Bike (Women)
Susan De Matti   Bronze

Kilometer Time Trial (Men)
Erin Hartwell   Silver

Match Sprint (Men)
Marty Nothstein   Silver

2

Meet the U.S. Cycling Teams

Mountain Bike Team

BROWN, TRAVIS

Height: 6' 1"

Weight: 165 lb

Born: Aug. 7, 1969

Hometown: Durango, CO

Residence: Boulder, CO

Discipline: Cross-country, cyclo-cross

Team: Trek-Volkswagen

- Olympics: 2000
- World Mountain Bike Championships: 1990, 1995, 1997-99
- National cross-country champion: 1999
- National race wins: four (cross-country)

2000   UCI **World Ranking** (Aug. 21): 85th
UCI **World Cup Series:** 48th (July 9)

20th, Mont-Sainte-Anne, Quebec, Canada
20th, Canmore, Alberta, Canada
48th, Napa, CA
**Chevy Trucks NORBA National Championship Series
(cross-country)**: 6th overall
4th, Deer Valley, UT
8th, Crystal Mountain, WA
10th, Mount Snow, VT
**Chevy Trucks NORBA National Championship Series
(short-track cross-country)**: 35th overall
17th, Mount Snow, VT
18th, Deer Valley, UT
Olympic Long Team Mountain Bike Qualifying Event
(Goodyear, AZ): 3rd

1999   World Mountain Bike Championships (Are, Sweden):
did not finish due to injury
UCI World Cup Series: 64th overall
16th, Sydney, Australia
26th, Napa, CA
**Chevy Trucks National Championship Series
(cross-country)**:1st overall
1st, Seven Springs, PA
2nd, Mount Snow, VT
4th, Snow Summit, CA
4th, Welch Village, MN
6th, Mammoth Mountain, CA
6th, Deer Valley, UT
**Chevy Trucks National Championship Series
(short-track cross-country)**: 8th overall
5th, Seven Springs, PA
6th, Deer Valley, UT
7th, Mount Snow, VT
8th, Snow Summit, CA
10th, Welch Village, MN
SuperCup Cyclo-Cross Series (San Francisco): 8th
Mercury Tour (Steamboat, CO): 9th overall
Saturn USCF National Cyclo-Cross Championships
(San Francisco): 9th
SRAM Sea Otter Classic (Monterey, CA): 11th overall

DUNLAP, ALISON

Height: 5' 6"

Weight: 124 lb

Born: July 27, 1969

Hometown: Denver, CO

Residence: Colorado Springs, CO

Discipline: Cross-country, road, cyclo-cross

Team: GT

- Olympics: 1996 (road), 2000 (mountain bike)
- World Mountain Bike Championships: 1994, 1997-2000
- World Road Cycling Championships: 1993-94 (bronze), 1998-99
- World Cyclo-Cross Championships: 2000
- UCI World Cup wins (mtb): two (cross-country)
- National cross-country champion: 1999
- National short-track cross-country champion: 1999
- National cyclo-cross champion: 1997-99
- National Road and Omnium Collegiate champion: 1991
- National race wins: three (cross-country), four (short-track cross-country)

Unless otherwise noted, all races since the start of 1999 are mountain bike.

2000   UCI World Ranking - mtb (Aug. 21): 3rd
World Mountain Bike Championships (Sierra Nevada, Spain): 6th
World Cyclo-Cross Championships
(St. Michielsgestel, The Netherlands): 5th (top U.S. rider)
UCI World Cup Series: 2nd overall (July 9)
>   2nd, St. Wendel, Germany
>   32nd, Mazatlan, Mexico
>   2nd, Napa, CA
>   4th, Sarentino, Italy
>   4th, Houffalize, Belgium
>   4th, Mont-Sainte-Anne, Quebec, Canada
>   5th, Canmore, Alberta, Canada

Chevy Trucks NORBA National Championship Series
(cross-country): 44th overall
>   2nd, Mount Snow

Chevy Trucks NORBA National Championship Series
(short-track cross-country): 36th overall
  1st, Mount Snow, VT
Redlands (CA) Bicycle Classic: 1st, two stage race wins
Mercury Sea Otter Classic (Monterey, CA): 6th, one stage race win

1999 World Mountain Bike Championships (Are, Sweden): 4th
World Road Cycling Championships (Verona, Italy): team member
Pan American Games (Winnipeg, Manitoba, Canada): 1st
UCI World Cup Series: 4th overall
  1st, Napa, CA
  5th, San Lorenzo de El Escorial, Spain
  6th, Canmore, Alberta, Canada
  7th, Plymouth, Great Britain
  8th, Sydney, Australia
  10th, St. Wendel, Germany
  11th, Houffalize, Belgium
  12th, Snow Summit, CA
Chevy Trucks National Championship Series (cross-country):
1st overall
  1st, Mount Snow, VT
  1st, Welch Village, MN
  1st, Deer Valley, UT
  3rd, Mammoth Mountain, CA
Chevy Trucks National Championship Series
(short-track cross-country): 1st overall
  1st, Mount Snow, VT
  1st, Welch Village, MN
  1st, Deer Valley, UT
  2nd, Mammoth Mountain, CA
National Cyclo-Cross Championships (San Francisco): 1st
SuperCup Cyclo-Cross Series (San Francisco): 1st
SRAM Sea Otter Classic (Monterey, CA): 1st overall, two stage wins
IronHorse Classic (Durango, CO): 1st
Mercury Tour (Steamboat, CO): 2nd overall, three stage wins
Redlands (CA) Bicycle Classic (road): 2nd overall, one stage win
Hewlett-Packard International Women's Challenge (ID) - road:
4th overall

JUAREZ, DAVID "TINKER"

Height: 5' 8"

Weight: 145 lb

Born: March 4, 1961

Hometown: Norwalk, CA

Residence: Downey, CA

Discipline: Cross-country

Team: Volvo-Cannondale

- Olympics: 1996, 2000
- Pan American Games: 1995 (gold)
- World Mountain Bike Championships: 1993, 1994 (silver), 1995, 1997-2000
- National Cross-Country champion: 1994, 1995, 1998
- National race wins: one (cross-country)

2000 UCI World Ranking (Aug. 21): 50th
World Mountain Bike Championships (Sierra Nevada, Spain): team member
UCI World Cup Series: 37th overall, top American (July 9)
          10th, Mazatlan, Mexico
          22nd, Canmore, Alberta, Canada
          35th, Napa, CA
          45th, Houffalize, Belgium
Chevy Trucks NORBA National Championship Series (cross-country): 12th overall
          5th, Mount Snow, VT
          7th, Crystal Mountain, WA
          34th, Snow Summit, CA
Chevy Trucks NORBA National Championship Series (short-track cross-country): 36th overall
          19th, Crystal Mountain, WA
          23rd, Mount Snow, VT
Olympic Long Team Qualifying Event (Goodyear, AZ): 2nd

1999 World Mountain Bike Championships (Are, Sweden): 42nd
UCI World Cup Series: 39th overall

14th, Sydney, Australia
24th, Napa, CA
31st, Canmore, Alberta, Canada
38th, St. Wendel, Germany
40th, Snow Summit, CA
Chevy Trucks National Championship Series
(cross-country) 9th overall
5th, Welch Village, MN
10th, Mount Snow, VT
12th, Seven Springs, PA
13th, Snow Summit, CA
14th, Deer Valley, UT
Chevy Trucks National Championship Series
(short-track cross-country): 5th overall
3rd, Deer Valley, UT
5th, Seven Springs, PA
9th, Mount Snow, VT
SRAM Sea Otter Classic (Monterey, CA): 6th overall
Redlands (CA) Bicycle Classic - road: 27th overall

MATTHES, RUTHIE

Height: 5' 5"

Weight: 126 lb

Born: Nov. 11, 1965

Hometown: Ketchum, ID

Residence: Durango, CO

Discipline: Cross-country

Team: Trek-Volkswagen

- Olympics: 2000
- World Mountain Bike Championships: 1990 (bronze),1991 (gold), 1992 (silver), 1993 (bronze), 1994-95, 1996 (silver), 1997-2000
- World Cyclo-Cross Championships: 2000
- World Road Cycling Championships: 1990 (silver), 1991
- UCI World Cup champion: 1992

- UCI World Cup race wins: three
- National Cross-Country champion: 1996-98
- National race wins: 11 (cross-country)

2000 UCI World Ranking - mtb (Aug. 21): 9th
World Mountain Bike Championships (Sierra Nevada, Spain):
16th (cross-country); 7th (team relay)
World Cyclo-Cross Championships (St. Michielsgestel,
The Netherlands): 13th
UCI World Cup Series: 9th overall (July 9)
    6th, Sarentino, Italy
    6th, Mont-Sainte-Anne, Quebec, Canada
    8th, Mazatlan, Mexico
    9th, Canmore, Alberta, Canada
    12th, Napa, CA
    19th, Houffalize, Belgium
    20th, St. Wendel, Germany
**Chevy Trucks NORBA National Championship Series
(cross-country):** 2nd overall
    2nd, Deer Valley, UT
    2nd, Snow Summit, CA
    3rd, Mount Snow, VT
    5th, Crystal Mountain, WA
Wetzikon Invitational (Switzerland - cyclo-cross): 6th
Redlands (CA) Bicycle Classic - road: 20th

1999 World Mountain Bike Championships (Are, Sweden): 11th
Diesel/UCI Cross-Country World Cup Series: 12th overall
    5th, Snow Summmit, CA
    8th, Canmore, Alberta, Canada
    9th, Houfallize, Belgium
    11th, Napa, CA
    12th, San Lorenzo de El Escorial, Spain
    15th, St. Wendel, Germany
    16th, Sydney, Australia
    18th, Plymouth, Great Britain
Chevy Trucks National Championship Series (cross-country):
2nd overall
    1st, Mammoth Mountain, CA
    2nd, Welch Village, MN
    3rd, Mount Snow, VT
    3rd, Seven Springs, PA

5th, Deer Valley, UT
Chevy Trucks National Championship Series
(short-track cross-country): 2nd overall
2nd, Deer Valley, UT
3rd, Mammoth Mountain, CA
3rd, Seven Springs, PA
3rd, Mount Snow, VT
4th, Welch Village, MN
National Cyclo-Cross Championships (San Francisco): 6th
Mercury Tour (Steamboat, CO): 2nd
SuperCup Cyclo-Cross Series (San Francisco): 5th
SRAM Sea Otter Classic (Monterey, CA): 6th

TROMBLEY, ANN

Height: 5' 3"

Weight: 125 lb

Born: Nov. 22, 1963

Hometown: San Anselmo, CA

Residence: Golden, CO

Discipline: Cross-country

Team: Team Koulius Zaard

- Olympics: 2000
- World Mountain Bike Championships: 1998-2000
- National race wins: one (cross-country)

2000   UCI World Ranking (Aug. 21): 13th
World Mountain Bike Championships (Sierra Nevada, Spain): 12th
UCI World Cup Series: 12th overall (July 9)
7th, Sarentino, Italy
10th, Canmore, Alberta, Canada
10th, Houffalize, Belgium
14th, Mazatlan, Mexico
15th, St. Wendel, Germany
16th, Napa, CA
20th, Mont-Sainte-Anne, Quebec, Canada

Chevy Trucks NORBA National Championship Series
(cross-country): 6th overall
>   3rd, Snow Summit, CA
>   7th, Mount Snow, VT
>   8th, Crystal Mountain, WA
>   11th, Deer Valley, UT

Chevy Trucks NORBA National Championship Series
(short-track cross-country): 4th overall
>   2nd, Snow Summit, CA
>   5th, Deer Valley, UT
>   6th, Mount Snow, VT

Olympic Long Team Qualifying Event (Goodyear, AZ): 1st
Redlands (CA) Bicycle Classic - road: 36th

1999 World Mountain Bike Championships (Are, Sweden): 20th

UCI World Cup Series: 32nd overall
>   11th, Snow Summit, CA
>   13th, Canmore, Alberta, Canada
>   24th, Napa, CA

Chevy Trucks National Championship Series (cross-country):
3rd overall
>   1st, Snow Summit, CA
>   3rd, Deer Valley, UT
>   4th, Seven Springs, PA
>   5th, Welch Village, MN
>   8th, Mammoth Mountain, CA
>   10th, Mount Snow, VT

Chevy Trucks National Championship Series
(short-track cross-country): 6th overall
>   3rd, Deer Valley, UT
>   5th, Seven Springs, PA
>   5th, Welch Village, MN
>   13th, Mount Snow, VT

Mercury Tour (Steamboat, CO): 4th
SuperCup Cyclo-Cross Series (Boulder, CO): 4th
National Cyclo-Cross Championships (San Francisco): 11th
SRAM Sea Otter Classic (Monterey, CA): 17th

Road Bike Team

ARMSTRONG, LANCE

Height: 5' 10"

Weight: 165 lb

Born: Sept. 18, 1971

Hometown: Austin, TX

Residence: Austin, TX/ Nice, France

Team: United States Postal Service

- Olympics: 1992, 1996, 2000
- Tour de France champion: 1999, 2000
- World Professional Road Race champion: 1993
- World Road Cycling Championships: 1990-91, 1993-94; 1998
- World Junior Road Cycling Championships: 1989
- National Road Cycling champion: 1991 (road race)
- Junior National Road Cycling champion: 1990 (individual time trial, team time trial)
- U.S. National Team: 1991-92, 1998-99
- Winner of the Arete Award for Courage in Sport for his miraculous recovery to the elite level of cycling after being diagnosed with testicular cancer in October 1996

2000   Tour de France: 1st; won stage 19
King of the Mountain: 6th
UCI World rankings: 5th
GP Eddy Merckx (Belgium): 1st
           (teamed with Viatcheslav Ekimov of Russia)
Paris-Camembert (France): 2nd (top U.S. rider)
Classique des Alpes (France): 3rd (top U.S. rider)
Dauphine Libere (France): 3rd, won mountain jersey
GP Kanton Aargau/GP Gippingen (Switzerland): 4th (top U.S. rider)
World Cup (Zurich, Switzerland): 5th (top U.S. rider)
Gran Premio Miguel Indurain (Spain): 7th (top U.S. rider)

Amstel Gold Race (Netherlands): 39th (top U.S. rider)
Setmana Catalana (Spain): 51st
Tour of Burgos (Spain): 69th

1999 **UCI World Road Ranking:** 7th (top U.S. rider)
Tour de France: 1st; won prologue, won stages 8, 9, and 19
Boxmeer Criterium (Netherlands): 1st
Amstel Gold Race (Netherlands): 2nd
BMC Software Downtown Criterium (Austin, TX): 2nd
Vuelta Ciclista Aaragon (Spain): 7th; one stage race win
Route de Sud (France): one stage race win
Circuit de la Sarthe (France): one stage race win
Chevy Trucks National Championship Series (Mount Snow, VT):
4th, short-track cross-country - MTB
6th, cross-country - MTB
King of the Rockies Series (Winter Park, CO - MTB): 2nd

CRUZ, ANTONIO

Height: 5' 9 1/2"

Weight: 140 lb

Born: Oct. 31, 1971

Hometown: Whittier, CA

Residence: Long Beach, CA

Team: Saturn

- U.S. Olympic Trials champion: 2000 (road race)
- USPRO National Criterium champion: 1999

2000 **U.S. Olympic Team Trials for Road Cycling** (Jackson, MS): 1st
U.S. Postal Service USPRO National Criterium Championship
(Downers Grove, IL): 3rd
USCF National Road Cycling Championships/Tour LeFleur
(Jackson, MS): 15th, individual time trial
BMC Software Tour of San Jose: 3rd

McLane Pacific Bicycle Classic (Merced, CA): 3rd, criterium, road race
BMC Software Tour of Houston: 4th
Manhattan Beach Grand Prix (CA): 4th
Wendy's International Cycling Classic (OH): 4th
Chris Thater Memorial Criterium (Binghamton, NY): 5th
Wine Country Classic (Santa Rosa, CA): 5th, criterium
First Charter Criterium (Shelby, NC): 6th
BMC Software Downtown Criterium (Austin, TX): 7th
Tour de 'Toona (PA): 8th
Tour of Willamette (OR): 8th
Xcelerate Twilight Criterium (Athens, GA): 10th
TDK Nevada City Bicycle Classic (CA): 10th
Solano Bicycle Classic (CA): 10th, one stage race win
First Union Classic (Trenton, NJ): 12th
U.S. Postal Service Clarendon Cup (Arlington, VA): 12th
First Union USPRO Championship (Philadelphia, PA): 13th
Tour of Langkawi (Malaysia): 16th; one stage race win
Mercury Sea Otter Classic (Monterey, CA): 16th
Tour of the Gila (NM): 16th
Dayton Pro/Am (OH): won sprinters jersey, King of the Mountain

1999 USPRO National Criterium Championships (Downers Grove, IL): 2nd; top U.S. rider - national champion
Killington Stage Race (VT): 4th
Manhattan Beach Grand Prix (CA): 4th
Cascade Cycling Classic (OR): 5th
BMC Software Tour of Houston: 7th
Chris Thater Memorial Criterium (Binghamton, NY): 8th
Red Zinger Classic (CO): 8th
USCF National Racing Calendar standings: 17th

FREEDMAN, NICOLE

Height: 5' 2"

Weight: 115 lb

Born: May 21, 1972

Hometown: Newton, MA

Residence: Stanford, CA

Team: Charles Schwab

- Olympics: 2000
- Olympic Trials champion: 2000 (road race)
- National Road Cycling champion: 2000 (road race)
- National Collegiate Road Cycling champion: 1994 (team time trial)
- U.S. National Team: 1997

2000   U.S. Olympic Team Trials for Road Cycling (Jackson, MS):
1st, road race
USCF Elite National Criterium Championship
(Downers Grove, IL): 3rd
Another Dam Race (Parker, AZ): 1st, road race
U.S. Postal Service Clarendon Cup (Arlington, VA): 2nd
BMC Software Tour of San Jose: 3rd
Trophée International (France): 34th
HP LaserJet Women's Challenge (ID): 66th; 3rd, sprinters jersey

1999   Wendy's International Cycling Classic (WI): 1st;
one stage race win
Manhattan Beach Grand Prix (CA): 1st
Another Dam Race (Parker, AZ): 2nd, one stage race win
Redlands Bicycle Classic (CA) : won sprint competition
and prologue
USCF National Racing Calendar standings: 14th
Saturn USPRO Tour ranking: 7th

HAMILTON, TYLER

Height: 5' 8"

Weight: 140 lb

Born: March 1, 1971

Hometown: Marblehead, MA

Residence: Boulder, CO

Team: United States Postal Service

- Olympics: 2000
- World Road Cycling Championships: 1994, 1996-98
- National Collegiate Road champion: 1993
- U.S. National Team: 1994, 1998

2000 UCI World rankings: 82nd
Tour de France: 25th
Tour of Holland: 4th, one stage race win (top U.S. rider)
GP Eddy Merckx (Belgium): 9th (teamed with Christian Vande Velde)
Tour of Burgos (Spain): 42nd
Criterium du Dauphiné Libéré (France): 1st, won two stage races, mountain jersey
Classique des Alpes (France): 9th
Liege-Bastogne-Liege (Belgium): 30th
Gran Premio Miguel Indurain (Spain): 44th
Amstel Gold Race (Netherlands): 65th
GP Kanton Aargau/GP Gippingen (Switzerland): 65th
Classica San Sebastian (Spain): 69th

1999 UCI World Road ranking: 101st
Mt. Washington Hill Climb (NH): 1st
Tour of Denmark: 1st, one stage race win
Circuit de la Sarthe (France): 5th
GP Eddy Merckx (Belgium): 7th
Tour de France: 13th
Luik-Bastenaken-Luik (World Cup IV, Belgium): 23rd
Setmana Catalana (Spain): 27th (top U.S. rider)
Amstel Gold Race (Netherlands): 45th

HINCAPIE, GEORGE

Height: 6' 3"

Weight: 185 lb

Born: June 29, 1973

Hometown: Charlotte, NC

Residence: Greenville, SC

Team: United States Postal Service

- Olympics: 1992, 1996, 2000
- World Road Cycling Championships: 1993, 1998
- Junior World Road Cycling Championships: 1990, 1991 (silver, team time trial)
- Junior World Track Cycling Championships: 1991 (bronze, individual pursuit)
- National Road Cycling champion: 1992 (team time trial)
- Junior National Road Cycling champion: 1989 (team time trial)
- Junior National Track Cycling champion: 1988-89 (omnium), 1991 (individual pursuit, team pursuit)
- U.S. National Team: 1991-93, 1998-99

2000 Tour de France: 65th
UCI World rankings: 80th
First Union USPRO Championships (Philadelphia, PA): 5th
First Union Classic (Trenton, NJ): 3rd
Trofeo Luis Puig (Spain): 4th (top U.S. rider)
Paris-Roubaix (France): 6th (top U.S. rider)
First Union Invitational (Lancaster, PA): 7th
10th RAI Amsterdam Dernyrace (The Netherlands): 16th
(top U.S. rider)
Tour of Holland: 16th
Tour of Flanders (World Cup - Belgium): 17th
First Union Wilmington Classic (DE): 23rd
Ghent-Wevelgem (Belgium): 26th
Tour of Luxembourg: 26th
Paris-Nice: 28th
Tour of Valencia (Spain): 48th (top U.S. rider)

Classica San Sebastian (Spain): 59th
1999 UCI World Road ranking: 50th
First Union Classic (Trenton, NJ): 1st
First Union Invitational (Lancaster, PA): 3rd
Paris-Roubaix (World Cup #3, France): 4th
Gent-Wevelgem (Belgium): 4th (top U.S. rider)
HEW Cyclassics (World Cup - Germany): 5th (top U.S. rider)
Tour of Denmark: 7th
Milan-San Remo (World Cup #1, Italy): 9th (top U.S. rider)
First Union USPRO Championship (Philadelphia, PA): 9th
Tour of Holland: 16th
Trofeo Luis Puig (Spain): 17th (top U.S. rider)
World Cup #2 (Belgium): 21st (top U.S. rider)
Scheldeprijs Schoten/GP de L'Escaut (Belgium): 24th (top U.S. rider)
Ruta Cicilista del Sol (Spain): 26th (top U.S. rider)
Three Days of Panne (Belgium): 33rd
Paris-Nice (France): 35th
Tour de France: 78th; 7th, sprinter jersey
Tour of Britain: one stage race win
Saturn USPRO Tour standings: 12th

HOLDEN, MARI

Height: 5' 4"

Weight: 130 lb

Born: March 30, 1971

Hometown: Ventura, CA

Residence: Colorado Springs, CO

Team: Timex

- Olympics: 2000
- World Road Cycling Championships: 1995-99
- National Road Cycling champion: 1995-96 (individual time trial), 1998 (individual time trial), 1999 (road race, individual time trial), 2000 (individual time trial)
- U.S. National Team: 1996-99

2000 U.S. Olympic Team Trials for Road Cycling (Jackson, MS): 26th, road race
USCF National Road Cycling Championships/Tour LeFleur (Jackson, MS): 1st, individual time trial
UCI World rankings: 29th (top U.S. rider)
Thringen Rundfahrt (Germany): 9th
Trophée International (France): 10th
World Cup #1 (Canberra, Australia): 21st
World Cup #5 (Montreal): 25th
Tour of the Gila (NM): 1st
Tour of Willamette (OR): 1st; two stage race wins
Mercury Sea Otter Classic (Monterey, CA): 2nd (top U.S. rider)
Zinger Cycling Challenge (Breckenridge, CO): 2nd
Tour de Snowy (Australia): 4th (top U.S. rider)
Canberra-Cooma Classic (Canberra, Australia - road): 13th
First Union Liberty Classic (Philadelphia, PA): 23rd

1999 UCI World Road Rankings: 15th (top U.S. rider)
World Road Cycling Championships (Treviso/Verona, Italy): 18th, individual time trial; dnf, road race
USCF National Road Cycling Championships (Cincinnati, OH): 1st, road race, time trial
HP LaserJet Women's Challenge (ID): 2nd (top U.S. rider); won sprinters jersey; one stage race win; 2nd, overall points; 3rd, sprint points
Pan American Games (Winnipeg, Canada): 3rd, individual time trial
Street Skills Women's Cycle Classic (New Zealand): 4th
Tour de Snowy (New Zealand): 7th; one stage race win; 7th, mountain points
La Grande Boucle Féminine (Tour de France): 8th; team, 1st
World Cup #4 (Belgium): 8th
Trophée International (France): 9th
World Cup #1 (Canberra, Australia): 11th
World Cup #2 (Hamilton, New Zealand): 20th
World Cup #4 (Montreal, Que., Canada): 18th
First Union Liberty Classic (Philadelphia, PA): 23rd
EDS Track Cup #3 (Blaine, MN): 5th, individual pursuit
USCF National Racing Calendar standings: 14th

KURRECK, KAREN

Height: 5' 6"

Weight: 125 lb

Born: June 13, 1962

Hometown: Cupertino, CA

Residence: Los Altos Hills, CA

Team: Eldisavino (Italy)

* Olympics: 2000
* World Road Cycling Championships: 1993, 1994 (gold, individual time trial); 1995-99
* USPRO National champion: 1997
* U.S. National Team: 1994-98

2000 U.S. Olympic Team Trials for Road Cycling (Jackson, MS): 16th, road race
USCF National Road Cycling Championships/Tour LeFleur (Jackson, MS): 2nd, individual time trial
U.S. Olympic Trials for Track Cycling/EDS Track Cup #2 (Frisco, TX): 1st, individual pursuit
UCI World rankings: 46th
Thuringen Rundfahrt (Germany): 10th
World Cup #1 (Canberra, Australia): 11th (top U.S. rider)
HP LaserJet Women's Challenge (ID): 7th; one stage race win (top U.S. rider)
BMC Software Tour of San Jose: 10th
La Fleche Wallonne/Waalse Pijl (Belgium): 13th (top U.S. rider)
Tour de Snowy (Australia): 17th
First Union Liberty Classic (Philadelphia, PA): 26th
La Primavera de Rosa (World Cup #2 - Milan, Italy): 48th (top U.S. rider)

1999 UCI World Road Rankings: 29th
World Road Cycling Championships (Verona, Italy): 33rd, road race (top U.S. rider)
Giro Del Piave (Italy): 1st

Tour de Snowy (New Zealand): 2nd; two stage race wins;
3rd, mountain points
World Cup #1 (Canberra, Australia): 6th
Haute Garrone (Italy): 6th
Tour of Switzerland: 14th
Tour of Mallorca (Spain): 15th
World Cup #2 (Hamilton, New Zealand): 17th

RODRIGUEZ, FRED

Height: 5' 10"

Weight: 155 lb

Born: July 3, 1973

Hometown: Charlotte, NC

Residence: Emeryville, CA

Team: Mapei-Quick Step (Italy)

- Olympics: 2000
- World Road Cycling Championships: 1993, 1995, 1999
- Junior World Road Cycling Championships:1991 (silver, team time trial)
- USPRO champion: 2000 (road race)
- Junior National Road Cycling champion: 1991 (road race, team time trial)
- U.S. National Team: 1993-95

2000 Tour de France: 86th
UCI World rankings: 68th
First Union USPRO Championships (Philadelphia, PA): 2nd (top U.S. rider)
First Union Classic (Trenton, NJ): 1st
International Niedersachsen Rundfarht (Germany): 2nd; one stage race win (top U.S. rider)
UNIQA Classic (Austria): 3rd, one stage race win (top U.S. rider)
First Union Invitational (Lancaster, PA): 3rd
Four Days of Dunkirk (France): 10th, one stage race win
First Union Wilmington Classic (DE): 10th
GP Kanton Aargau/GP Gippingen (Germany): 21st

Tour of Holland: 44th
Tour of Switzerland: 48th; one stage race win; won points jersey
(top U.S. rider)

1999   UCI World Road ranking: 192nd
World Road Cycling Championships (Verona, Italy): team member
Schaal Sels (Belgium): 1st
Volto de Algarne (Portugal): 5th (top U.S. rider)
First Union USPRO Championship: (Philadelphia, PA): 6th
Trans Canada Cycling Tour: 7th, won one stage race
Giro del Piemonte (Italy): 8th (top U.S. rider)
Manhattan Beach Grand Prix (CA): 10th
First Union Classic (Trenton, NJ): 13th
First Union Invitational (Lancaster, PA): 20th
Tour of Langkawi (Malaysia): 24th; one stage race win
Christiana Care Cup (Wilmington, DE): 29th

Track Bike Team

ARRUE, MARCELO

Height: 5' 9"

Weight: 180 lb

Born: Jan. 8, 1969

Hometown: Woodland Hills, CA

Residence: Woodland Hills, CA

Team: Team UPS

- Olympics: 2000
- World Track Cycling Championships: 1994-99
- National Track Cycling champion: 1995 (tandem sprint); 1999-2000 (Olympic Sprint)
- Junior National Track Cycling champion: 1983-84, 1986
- U.S. National Team: 1996-1999

2000 U.S. Olympic Team Trials for Track Cycling (Frisco, TX): 1st, Olympic Sprint; 2nd, Keirin; 5th, match sprint
EDS Elite National Track Cycling Championships/EDS Track Cup #4 (Colorado Springs, CO): 1st, Olympic Sprint; 2nd, Keirin; 3rd, match sprint
World Track Cup #3 (Mexico City): 5th, Keirin; 8th, Olympic Sprint
World Track Cup #2 (Cali, Colombia): 7th, match sprint, Olympic Sprint
Barbados Grand Prix: 2nd, match sprint, 200m time trial, 1,500m scratch race; 3rd, Keirin; 5th, Olympic Sprint
EDS Track Cup standings: 4th, sprint

1999 World Track Cycling Championships (Berlin, Germany): 11th, Olympic Sprint; 24th, match sprint
Pan American Games (Winnipeg, Canada): 1st, Olympic Sprint; 2nd, match sprint
EDS Elite National Track Cycling Championships (Trexlertown, PA): 1st, Olympic Sprint; 2nd, Keirin, match sprint
World Track Cup #5 (Cali, Colombia): 3rd, match sprint, Keirin; 4th, Olympic Sprint
World Track Cup #3 (Valencia, Spain): 4th, Keirin; 11th, match sprint
EDS World Cup of Cycling (Frisco, TX): 5th, sprint; 7th, Olympic Sprint
World Cup #1 (Mexico City): 4th, Olympic Sprint; 5th, sprint
EDS Track Cup #1 (San Jose, CA): 1st, sprint; Keirin; Italian pursuit
EDS Track Cup #2 (Frisco, TX): 2nd, sprint; 6th, Keirin
EDS Track Cup #3 (Blaine, MN): 1st, Keirin; 2nd, sprint, Olympic Sprint
EDS Track Cup standings: 1st, sprint

BAIROS, JOHN

Height: 5' 6"

Weight: 165 lb

Born: Nov. 8, 1977

Hometown: Redlands, CA

Residence: Redlands, CA

Team: Team UPS

- Olympics: 2000
- World Track Cycling Championships: 1999
- National Track Cycling champion: 1999-2000 (Olympic Sprint)
- U.S. National Team: 1998-99

2000 U.S. Olympic Team Trials for Track Cycling (Frisco, TX): 1st, Olympic Sprint; 5th, Keirin; 10th, match sprint
EDS Elite National Track Cycling Championships/EDS Track Cup #4 (Colorado Springs, CO): 1st, Olympic Sprint
World Track Cup #3 (Mexico City): 10th, match sprint
World Track Cup #2 (Cali, Colombia): 7th, Olympic Sprint
Copa Cuba Invitational (Havana): 1st, Olympic Sprint; 2nd, match sprint
EDS Track Cup standings: 17th, sprint

1999 World Track Cycling Championships (Berlin, Germany): 11th, Olympic Sprint; 25th, match sprint
EDS Elite National Track Cycling Championships (Trexlertown, PA): 1st, Olympic Sprint; 4th, match sprint, Keirin
Pan American Games (Winnipeg, Canada): 1st, Olympic Sprint
World Track Cup #5 (Cali, Colombia): 4th, Olympic Sprint
EDS World Cup of Cycling (Frisco, TX): 7th, Olympic Sprint
World Track Cup #1 (Mexico City): 4th, Olympic Sprint
EDS Track Cup #1 (San Jose, CA): 1st, Italian pursuit; 6th, sprint; 11th, Keirin
EDS Track Cup #2 (Frisco, TX): 5th, sprint; 7th, Keirin
EDS Track Cup standings: 4th, sprint

BOUCHARD-HALL, DEREK

Height: 6' 2"

Weight: 165 lb

Born: July 16, 1970

Hometown: Norton, MA

Residence: Palo Alto, CA

Team: Mercury

- Olympics: 2000
- USPRO National Criterium champion: 2000
- National Track Cycling champion: 2000 (team pursuit)
- World Track Cycling Championships: 1997-99
- U.S. National Team: 1998-99

2000 U.S. Olympic Team Trials for Road Cycling (Jackson, MS): 2nd, road race
U.S. Postal Service USPRO National Criterium Championships (Downers Grove, IL): 1st
EDS Elite National Track Cycling Championships (Colorado Springs, CO): 1st, team pursuit
World Cup #2 (Cali, Colombia - track): 3rd, team pursuit
Wine Country Classic (Santa Rosa, CA - road): 1st, criterium
Wendy's International Cycling Classic (OH - road): 7th
Xcelerate Twilight Criterium (Athens, GA - road): 7th
First Charter Criterium (Shelby, NC - road): 8th
First Union Wilmington Classic (DE - road): 9th
Tour de 'Toona (PA - road): 11th
Cascade Cycling Classic (OR - road): 23rd

1999 World Track Cycling Championships (Berlin, Germany): team member
Pan American Games (Winnipeg, Canada): 1st, team pursuit
Heart of It All Stage Race (OH - road): 1st
World Cup #1 (Mexico City - track): 3rd, team pursuit
Boulder-Roubaix (CO - road): 2nd
Wendy's International Cycling Classic (OH - road): 11th

BMC Software Downtown Criterium (Austin, TX - road): 16th
Fitchburg-Longsjo Classic (MA-road): 23rd, one stage race win
SRAM Sea Otter (CA - road): 38th
Trans Canada Cycling Tour (road): 64th
Tour of Willamette (OR - road): won prologue
USCF National Racing Calendar Standings: 24th

CARNEY, JAME

Height: 5' 8"

Weight: 150 lb

Born: Nov. 29, 1968

Hometown: Annandale, NJ

Residence: Durango, CO

Team: Shaklee

- Olympics: 1992, 2000
- World Track Cycling Championships: 1990-91, 1993, 1999
- Junior World Track Cycling Championships: 1986
- National Track Cycling champion: 1991 (team pursuit, points race, Madison), 1992 (team pursuit, points race), 1993 (Madison), 1996 (points race, Madison), 1998 (Madison), 1999 (Madison), 2000 (points race)
- Junior National Track Cycling champion: 1986
- National Collegiate Track champion: 1989-90, 1997
- U.S. National Team: 1987, 1992-94, 1998-99

2000   U.S. Olympic Team Trials for Track Cycling/EDS Track Cup #2 (Frisco, TX): 1st, points race, Madison, miss-and-out
EDS Elite National Track Cycling Championships/EDS Track Cup #4 (Colorado Springs, CO): 1st, points race; 2nd, team pursuit; 4th, individual pursuit
World Track Cup #3 (Mexico City): 4th, points race; 7th, Madison; 8th, Olympic Sprint
World Track Cup #1 (Moscow, Russia): 5th, points race
World Cup #4 (Turin, Italy): 11th, points race
EDS Elite National Track Cycling Championships (Colorado Springs, CO): 4th, individual pursuit

EDS Track Cup #1 (San Jose, CA): 1st, points race; scratch race; 2nd, Keirin
Superweek International Cycling Classic (WI): one stage race win
UCI World Track Cup rankings: 8th, points race
EDS Track Cup standings: 2nd, endurance

1999 World Track Cycling Championships (Berlin, Germany): 9th, points race
Pan American Games (Winnipeg, Canada): 2nd, Madison; 6th, points race
EDS Elite National Track Cycling Championships (Trexlertown, PA): 1st, Madison; 2nd, team pursuit; 5th, individual pursuit
World Cup #5 (Cali, Colombia): 6th, points race; 9th, Madison
World Cup #3 (Valencia, Spain): 10th, points race
World Cup #1 (Mexico City): 2nd, points race; 3rd, team pursuit
Oceania International Cycling Grand Prix (Sydney, Australia): 1st, points race; 4th, Madison; 10th, Olympic Sprint
EDS Track Cup #1 (San Jose, CA): 1st, scratch race; 2nd, points race, Italian pursuit; 4th, sprint
EDS Track Cup #2 (Frisco, TX): 1st, scratch race, miss-and-out; 2nd, points race
EDS Track Cup #3 (Blaine, MN): 1st, individual pursuit, team pursuit; Madison
EDS Track Cup standings: 1st, endurance

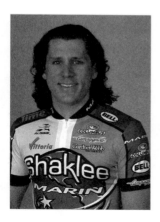

CARNEY, JONAS

Height: 5' 9"

Weight: 156 lb

Born: Feb. 3, 1971

Hometown: Annandale, NJ

Residence: Pacifica, CA

Team: Shaklee

- Olympics: 2000
- Junior World Track Cycling Championships: 1988-89

- National Track Cycling champion: 1990 (team pursuit), 1991 (Madison), 1993 (Madison), 1996 (Madison), 1997 (kilometer time trial), 1998 (points race, Madison), 1999 (kilometer time trial), 2000 (kilometer time trial, Olympic Sprint)
- National Road Cycling Championships: 1993 (criterium)
- Junior National Track Cycling Championships: 1987 (omnium), 1988 (kilometer time trial), 1989 (points race)
- Junior National Road Cycling Championships: 1987 (criterium), 1988 (road race, criterium), 1989 (road race)
- U.S. National Team: 1990-93, 1998

2000 U.S. Olympic Trials for Track Cycling (Frisco, TX): 2nd, kilometer time trial, Olympic Sprint
EDS Elite National Track Cycling Championships/EDS Track Cup #4 (Colorado Springs, CO): 1st, kilometer time trial, Olympic Sprint
World Track Cup #3 (Mexico City): 5th, kilometer time trial; 8th, Olympic Sprint
World Track Cup #1 (Moscow, Russia): 11th, Olympic Sprint; 12th, kilometer time trial
First Charter Criterium (Shelby, NC - road): 1st
Tour of Somerville (NJ - road): 1st
U.S. Postal Service Clarendon Cup (Arlington, VA): 2nd
Wine Country Classic (Santa Rosa, CA - road): 2nd, criterium
BMC Software Downtown Criterium (Austin, TX - road): 4th
BMC Software Tour of San Jose (road): 6th
BMC Software Tour of Houston (road): 10th
Xcelerate Twilight Criterium (Athens, GA - road): 15th
EDS Track Cup #1 (San Jose, CA): 6th, chariot race; 18th, points race
EDS Track Cup standings: 7th, sprint

1999 EDS Elite National Track Cycling Championships (Trexlertown, PA): 1st, kilometer time trial; 2nd, team pursuit; 3rd, Madison; 7th, points race
USPRO National Criterium Championship (Downers Grove, IL - road): 8th
World Cup #5 (Cali, Colombia - track): 5th, kilometer time trial
World Cup #3 (Valencia, Spain - track): 6th, kilometer time trial
EDS Track Cup #1 (San Jose, CA): 2nd, Italian pursuit
BMC Software Tour of Houston (road): 1st
Wine Country Classic (Santa Rosa, CA - road): 1st, criterium
First Charter Criterium (Shelby, NC): 1st
U.S. Postal Service Clarendon Cup (Arlington, VA): 3rd

Manhattan Beach Grand Prix (CA): 3rd
BMC Software Downtown Crtierium (Austin, TX): 4th
Golden Pantry Twilight Criterium (Athens, GA): 4th
Tour of Somerville (NJ): 8th
Chris Thater Memorial Criterium (Binghamton, NY): 17th
Saturn USPRO Tour standings (road): 7th
EDS Track Cup standings: 13th, endurance
USCF National Racing Calendar standings: 15th

CASEY, DYLAN
Height: 5' 8"
Weight: 140 lb
Born: April 13, 1971
Hometown: Walnut Creek, CA
Residence: Mountain View, CA / Spain
Team: United States Postal Service

- Olympics: 2000
- World Track Cycling Championships: 1998-99
- World Road Cycling Championships: 1998
- National Track Cycling champion: 1998 (individual pursuit)
- National Road Cycling champion: 1998 (individual time trial)
- U.S. National Team: 1999

2000 U.S. Olympic Team Trials for Road Cycling (Jackson, MS): 5th, road race
World Cup #2 (Cali, Colombia - track): 1st, individual pursuit; 3rd, team pursuit
Four Days of Dunkirk (France): 9th (top U.S. rider), one stage race win
Mercury Sea Otter Classic (Monterey, CA): 12th
Redlands Bicycle Classic (CA) : 44th, one stage race win
Three Days of Panne (Belgium - road): 53rd (top U.S. rider)
Tour of Luxembourg: 71st, one stage race win
GP Kanton Aargau/GP Gippingen (Switzerland): 75th

Tour of Aragon (Spain): 83rd
UCI World Track Cup rankings: 6th, individual pursuit

FRIEDICK, MARIANO

Height: 6' 2"

Weight: 178 lb

Born: Jan. 9, 1975

Hometown: Santa Monica, CA

Residence: Brentwood, CA

Team: Jelly Belly

* Olympics: 1996, 2000
* World Track Cycling Championships: 1994 (silver, team pursuit), 1995 (bronze, team pursuit), 1996-99
* Junior World Road Cycling Championships: 1993 (silver, road race)
* Junior World Track Cycling Championships: 1992, 1993
* National Track Cycling champion: 1993-94 (team pursuit), 1995 (individual pursuit, team pursuit, points race), 1998 (team pursuit), 2000 (team pursuit)
* Junior National Track Cycling champion: 1991 (omnium), 1993 (team pursuit)
* Junior National Road Cycling champion: 1993 (team time trial)
* U.S. National Team: 1994-99

2000 EDS Elite National Track Cycling Championships (Colorado Springs, CO): 1st, team pursuit
BMC Software Tour of Houston (road): 11th
Wendy's International Cycling Classic (OH - road): 13th
Tour of Normandy (France - road): 63rd

1999 World Track Cycling Championships (Berlin, Germany): 9th, team pursuit; 18th, individual pursuit
Pan American Games (Winnipeg, Canada): 1st, team pursuit
Open Des Nations (Paris, France): 2nd, team pursuit, individual pursuit
World Cup #5 (Cali, Colombia): 3rd, individual pursuit

HARTWELL, ERIN

Height: 6' 0"

Weight: 175 lb

Born: June 1, 1969

Hometown: Indianapolis, IN

Residence: Indianapolis, IN

Team: Saturn

- Olympics: 1992 (bronze, kilometer time trial), 1996 (silver, kilometer time trial), 2000
- World Track Cycling Championships: 1991, 1993, 1994 (silver, kilometer time trial), 1995 (bronze, kilometer time trial, Olympic sprint), 1998 (bronze, kilometer time trial)
- National Track Cycling champion: 1989-90 (kilometer time trial), 1992 (kilometer time trial, tandem sprint), 1993-94 (kilometer time trial), 1996 (kilometer time trial, Olympic sprint), 1997 (Olympic sprint), 1998 (kilometer time trial, Olympic sprint); 2000 (team pursuit)
- U.S. National Team: 1990-1999
- Junior National Track Cycling champion: 1987 (kilometer time trial)

2000 U.S. Olympic Team Trials for Track Cycling (Frisco, TX): 1st, individual pursuit; 3rd, points race; 6th, Madison
EDS Elite National Track Cycling Championships/EDS Track Cup #4 (Colorado Springs, CO): 1st, team pursuit
World Track Cup #2 (Cali, Colombia): 3rd, team pursuit
Dayton Pro/Am (OH - road): 2nd; one stage race win
GP Rennes (France - road): 17th (top U.S. rider)
Wendy's International Cycling Classic (OH - road): 19th; one stage race win
EDS Track Cup standings: 8th, endurance

1999 Pan American Games (Winnipeg, Canada): 2nd, kilometer time trial
EDS Track Cup #3 (Blaine, MN): 1st, Olympic sprint; 2nd, Madison

LINDENMUTH, TANYA

Height: 5' 1"

Weight: 135 lb

Born: May 25, 1979

Hometown: Trexlertown, PA

Residence: Trexlertown, PA

Team: Team UPS

- Olympics: 2000
- World Track Cycling Championships: 1999
- Junior World Track Cycling Championships: 1997
- National Track Cycling champion: 1999-2000 (500m time trial, match sprint)
- Junior National Track Cycling champion: 1997 (omnium, 500m time trial, match sprint)
- U.S. National Team: 1998

2000   U.S. Olympic Team Trials for Track Cycling/EDS Track Cup #2 (Frisco, TX): 1st, match sprint; 3rd, 500m time trial
EDS Elite National Track Cycling Championships/EDS Track Cup #4 (Colorado Springs, CO): 1st, match sprint, 500m time trial
World Cup #3 (Mexico City): 2nd, match sprint
World Cup #2 (Cali, Colombia): 2nd, match sprint
Copa Cuba Invitational (Havana): 1st, match sprint; 2nd, 500m time trial
UCI World Track Cup rankings: 3rd, match sprint
EDS Track Cup standings: 3rd, sprint

1999   World Track Cycling Championships (Berlin, Germany): 15th, match sprint
EDS Elite National Track Cycling Championships (Trexlertown, PA): 1st, match sprint, 500m time trial
World Cup #5 (Cali, Colombia): 3rd, match sprint; 8th, 500m time trial
World Cup #4 (Fiorenzuola d'Arda, Italy): 6th, match sprint

Oceania International Cycling Grand Prix (Sydney, Australia): 4th, match sprint; 5th, 500m time trial
GP Cottbus (Germany): 1st, match sprint
GP St. Denis (France): 3rd, match sprint
EDS Track Cup #3 (Blaine, MN): 3rd, match sprint; 4th, 500m time trial
EDS Track Cup #2 (Frisco, TN): 5th, match sprint; 7th, chariot race
EDS Track Cup #1 (San Jose, CA): 1st, Italian pursuit; 3rd, match sprint; 7th, Keirin
Copa Cuba: 4th, match sprint
EDS Track Cup standings: 2nd, sprint

MULKEY, TOMMY

Height: 6' 1"

Weight: 180 lb

Born: Oct. 16, 1972

Hometown: Griffin, GA

Residence: Athens, GA

Team: Zaxby's Cycling Team

- Olympics: 2000
- World Track Cycling Championships: 1997-99
- National Track Cycling champion: 1999 (individual pursuit, team pursuit), 2000 (team pursuit)
- National Collegiate Track Cycling champion: 1995 (individual pursuit)
- U.S. National Team: 1998-99

2000 EDS Elite National Track Cycling Championships (Colorado Springs, CO): 1st, team pursuit
World Cup #2 (Cali, Colombia): 3rd, team pursuit; 4th, Madison
Wendy's International Cycling Classic (OH - road): 39th

1999 World Track Cycling Championships (Berlin, Germany): 9th, team pursuit
Pan American Games (Winnipeg, Canada): 1st, team pursuit

EDS Elite National Track Cycling Championships (Trexlertown, PA): 1st, individual pursuit, team pursuit; 4th, Madison
World Cup #3 (Valencia, Spain): 7th, individual pursuit
EDS World Cup of Cycling (Frisco, TX): 3rd, team pursuit; 8th, Madison
World Track Cup #1 (Mexico City): 3rd, team pursuit; 8th, individual pursuit
Open Des Nations (Paris): 2nd, team pursuit
EDS Track Cup #2 (Frisco, TX): 6th, points race
EDS Track Cup standings: 8th, endurance

NOTHSTEIN, MARTY

Height: 6' 2"
Weight: 175 lb
Born: Feb. 10, 1971
Hometown: Trexlertown, PA
Residence: Trexlertown, PA
Team: autotrader.com/Cox

- Olympics: 1996 (silver, match sprint), 2000
- World Track Cycling Championships: 1989-92, 1993 (silver, Keirin), 1994 (gold, match sprint, Keirin), 1995 (bronze, Olympic sprint), 1996 (gold, Keirin; silver, match sprint), 1997 (bronze, Keirin), 1998-99
- National Track Cycling champion: 1989-92 (tandem sprint), 1993 (match sprint, Keirin), 1994 (Keirin), 1996-2000 (match sprint, Olympic sprint, Keirin)
- Junior National Track Cycling champion: 1989-90 (match sprint)
- U.S. National Team: 1990, 1993-99

2000   U.S. Olympic Team Trials for Track Cycling (Frisco, TX): 1st, match sprint, Keirin; 2nd, Olympic Sprint
EDS Elite National Track Cycling Championships/EDS Track Cup #4 (Colorado Springs, CO): 1st, match sprint, Keirin, Olympic Sprint
World Cup #2 (Cali, Colombia): 1st, match sprint; 5th, Keirin
EDS Track Cup #1 (San Jose, CA): 1st, Keirin; Chariot race

UCI World Track Cup rankings: 6th, match sprint
EDS Track Cup standings: 1st, sprint
1999   World Track Cycling Championships (Berlin, Germany): 5th, match sprint; 6th, Keirin; 11th, Olympic Sprint
Pan American Games (Winnipeg, Canada): 1st, match sprint, Keirin, Olympic Sprint
EDS Elite National Track Cycling Championships (Trexlertown, PA): 1st, Keirin, match sprint; Olympic Sprint
EDS World Track Cup of Cycling (Frisco, TX): 2nd, match sprint; 4th, Keirin
World Track Cup #1 (Mexico City): 2nd, Keirin; 3rd, sprint; 4th, Olympic Sprint
EDS Track Cup #3 (Blaine, MN): 1st, match sprint, Olympic Sprint
EDS Track Cup #2 (Frisco, TX): 1st, Keirin, Olympic Sprint, match sprint
EDS Track Cup standings: 2nd, sprint

VANDE VELDE, CHRISTIAN

Height: 5' 11"

Weight: 160 lb

Born: May 22, 1976

Hometown: Lemont, IL

Residence: Boulder, CO

Team: United States Postal Service

- Olympics: 2000
- World Road Cycling Championships: 1998
- World Under-23 Road Cycling Championships: 1996-97
- World Track Cycling Championships: 1996-97, 1999
- Junior World Track Cycling Championships: 1994
- National Track Cycling champion: 1994 (points race), 1996 (team pursuit), 1997 (individual pursuit, team pursuit, Madison)
- U.S. National Team: 1995-99

2000   GP Eddy Merckx (Belgium): 9th (teamed with Tyler Hamilton)
Gran Premio Miguel Indurain (Spain): 17th
Liege-Bastogne-Liege (Belgium): 18th (top U.S. rider)
La Fleche Wallonne/Waalse Pijl (Belgium): 32nd (top U.S. rider)
Setmana Catalana (Spain): 32nd (top U.S. rider)
Paris-Nice: 39th
Pais Vasco (Spain): 48th (top U.S. rider)
Tour of Valencia (Spain): 53rd

1999   Tour de France: 85th; 11th, best youth
World Track Cycling Championships (Berlin, Germany): 9th, team pursuit; 14th, individual pursuit
USPRO National Criterium Championship (Downers Grove, IL): 10th
EDS World Cup of Cycling (Frisco, TX - track): 1st, individual pursuit; 3rd, team pursuit
Three Days of Dunkirk (France): 3rd (top U.S. rider)
Circuit de la Sarthe (France): 4th (top U.S. rider)
Redlands Bicycle Classic (CA): 1st
U.S. Postal Service Clarendon Cup (Arlington, VA): 9th
Tour of Denmark: 15th
First Union USPRO Championship (Philadelphia, PA): 27th
First Union Classic (Trenton, NJ): 30th
Fleche Wallone (Belgium): 31st
Setmana Catalana (Spain): 35th
Three Days of Panne (Belgium): 46th

VEENSTRA-MIRABELLA, ERIN

Height: 5' 5"

Weight: 141 lb

Born: May 18, 1978

Hometown: Racine, WI

Residence: Colorado Springs, CO

Team: Timex

• Olympics: 2000

- World Track Cycling Championships: 1998-99
- Junior World Track Cycling Championships: 1996
- National Track Cycling champion: 1998 (points race), 2000 (individual pursuit, points race)
- Junior National Track champion: 1992 (omnium), 1996 (points race, match sprint, 500m time trial)
- U.S. National Team: 1998-99

2000 U.S. Olympic Trials for Track Cycling/EDS Track Cup #2 (Frisco, TX): 3rd, individual pursuit; 4th, miss-and-out; 9th, points race
EDS Elite National Track Cycling Championships/EDS Track Cup #4 (Colorado Springs, CO): 1st, individual pursuit, points race
World Cup #1 (Canberra, Australia - road): 24th
World Cup #2 (Cali, Colombia): 4th, individual pursuit; 10th, points race
World Cup #4 (Turin, Italy): 7th, individual pursuit
EDS Track Cup #1 (San Jose, CA): 1st, points race, scratch race; 3rd, chariot race, Keirin
BMC Software Tour of Houston (road): 6th
Canberra-Cooma Classic (Canberra, Australia - road): 8th (top U.S. rider)
Wendy's International Cycling Classic (OH - road): 14th
Tour de Snowy (Australia - road): 37th
HP LaserJet Women's Challenge (ID - road): 47th; 7th, espoir
UCI World Track Cup rankings: 10th, individual pursuit
EDS Track Cup standings: 1st, endurance

1999 World Track Cycling Championships (Berlin, Germany): 6th, points race; 8th, individual pursuit
Pan American Games (Winnipeg, Canada): 1st, individual pursuit, points race
EDS Elite National Track Cycling Championships (Trexlertown, PA): 2nd, individual pursuit; 7th, points race
EDS World Cup of Cycling (Frisco, TX): 1st, individual pursuit; 5th, points race
World Track Cup #1 (Mexico City): 6th, points race; 7th, individual pursuit
EDS Track Cup #1 (San Jose, CA): 1st points race; 2nd, Italian pursuit; 4th, Keirin
EDS Track Cup #2 (Frisco, TX): 1st, points race; 5th, miss-and-out
EDS Track Cup #3 (Blaine, MN): 1st, individual pursuit; points race

SRAM Sea Otter Classic (Monterey, CA - road): 13th
Redlands Bicycle Classic (CA - road): 14th
Tour of Willamette (OR - road): 17th
HP LaserJet Women's Challenge (ID - road): 45th; 4th, espoir
EDS Track Cup standings: 1st, endurance

WITTY, CHRIS

Height: 5' 6"

Weight: 145 lb

Born: June 23, 1975

Hometown: West Allis, WI

Residence: Park City, UT

- Olympics (cycling): 2000
- Olympics (speed skating): 1994, 1998 (silver, 1,000m; bronze, 1,500m)
- World Speed Skating Championships: 1996
- World Track Cycling Championships: 1998
- Junior World Track Cycling Championships: 1991, 1992 (bronze, match sprint), 1993
- National Track Cycling champion: 1996, 1998 (500m time trial)
- Junior National Track Cycling champion: 1992 (match sprint)
- U.S. National Cycling Team: 1997-99

2000 U.S. Olympic Team Trials for Track Cycling/EDS Track Cup #2 (Frisco, TX): 2nd, 500m time trial
EDS Elite National Track Cycling Championships/EDS Track Cup #4 (Colorado Springs, CO): 3rd, 500m time trial, match sprint
World Track Cup #1 (Moscow, Russia): 7th, 500m time trial; 12th, match sprint
World Track Cup #3 (Mexico City): 5th, 500m time trial
UCI World Track Cup rankings: 11th, 500m time trial
EDS Track Cup standings: 4th, sprint

1999 Did not compete

3

A Brief History of Cycling

History indicates that the first functioning bicycle was designed in the fifteenth century by master craftsman and artisan Leonardo da Vinci. It was an odd-looking contraption, driven by cranks and pedals and held together with connecting rods. The first machine to resemble the contemporary bicycle was designed in France in the late eighteenth century. Known as the *celerifere*, this vehicle consisted of a wooden horse-shaped frame mounted on two wheels, propelled by the rider's feet. It was a cumbersome thing and difficult to mobilize, but it marked the beginning of modern bicycle construction.

Note the lack of pedals. This *celerifere* from the early 1800s was propelled by the rider's feet.

Nearly 20 years later, Baron Karl von Mannheim designed a "bicycle" with steering, which quickly became nicknamed the "dandy-horse." It wasn't too dandy for the French postal service, however, which used it to deliver mail in the countryside. Kirkpatrick McMillan, a Scot, put pedals and connecting rods together, and the result was an early version of what could be defined as a bicycle.

In the late 1860s, two Frenchmen, engineer Ernest Michaux and mechanic Pierre Lallement, gave the bicycle yet another look with the invention of the *velocipede*. The "bone shaker," as it was informally known, soon evolved into the high-wheeler.

Ernest Michaux with his *velocipede*

This enormous contraption, consisting of a 4-foot, 6-inch front wheel and a 17-inch rear wheel, remains one of the strongest visual images associated with sports of the late nineteenth century.

The high-wheeler's development coincided with one of the most significant improvements in cycling comfort: the air-filled rubber bicycle tire developed by Scot John Dunlop in 1887. Engineers discovered that the new rubber tire could be successfully mounted to a thin-spoked wheel. This construction allowed for easier steering and improved both mobility and control.

High-wheeler of 1885

As bicycles became easier to handle, women and children began to ride them as well. By 1880, cycling was not only the mass transit of choice, but the number-one form of family-oriented recreation. This interest created a vigorous business in the production and sale of cycling costumes and accessories similar to today's lively commerce in sports apparel.

Safety bicycle of 1893 with chain-wheel drive

Before the turn of the century, a low-wheeled bicycle—called a safety bicycle—was designed using a chain-wheel drive to the rear axle. It took some time for mechanics to refine this new design, and it did not come into popular use until after 1910. But with the invention of the chain-wheel drive, the era of the high-wheeler was over. Subsequently, bicycle design and construction evolved toward the lower, lighter-weight cycles we associate with the modern era.

Racing with the Wind

The 1880s were characterized by unbridled growth in recreational cycling, both in Western Europe and North America. The fun was absolutely contagious; everyone wanted to be outdoors riding. With such enthusiasm in the air, could a match race be far behind? Evidently not, as bicycle racing soon rivaled horse racing as the most popular weekend sport.

By 1885, professional cyclists roamed the countryside putting on exhibitions and challenging locals to a race. To imagine the popularity of their arrival, pretend the Tour de France was to take a side trip through your neighborhood—everyone would be out to see their heroes. And so it was in 1885. Cyclists, then as now, were international superstars and even began to receive corporate sponsorship.

Men's and women's cycling costumes of the 1870s.
Note that the lady is riding side-saddle.

Although cyclists were still a loose-knit group, there were attempts at organization. As a result, a sanctioned event was finally developed, and the first official cycling world championship took place in Buffalo, NY, in 1888, eight years before the first modern Olympic Games included cycling on its program.

At this time, road racing was the most common form of competition, but because of the poor condition of many roads, cyclists felt that tracks would be easier to negotiate, and racing times would be faster. By the end of the nineteenth century, there were cycling tracks all over Europe and a few in the United States. After experiments with wood, grit, and shale, cement tracks became the international standard.

In the 1890s, England was the hotbed of world cycling, with more than 700 factories producing 750,000 bicycles a year. But by 1900, the market was saturated, and many tracks and plants closed following the downturn in demand. To remedy this decline, the *Union Cycliste International* (UCI) was formed in 1900, and under its leadership, world cycling continued to progress.

Today, new developments in design and technology are occurring in countries throughout the world. As a result, many people assume cycling has always been as popular as it is now; but in truth, cycling, especially in the United States, has gone through some dramatic ups and downs.

Cycling in America

Since its invention in France in the late eighteenth century, cycling has retained its popularity with Western European nations, but American enthusiasm as been an on-again, off-again affair. In the 1920s, an age of remarkable prosperity, people cast aside their bicycles to indulge their newest passion, the automobile. During the 1930s, a time often referred to as the Great Depression, economics made bicycle transportation attractive once again. This situation continued through the war years, 1941-1945, when the supply of petroleum products was severely restricted. After World War II, the automobile once again became a major American preoccupation, and the bicycle again was cast aside. During the 1950s, mostly young people rode bicycles; adults, on the other hand, wanted to be seen in their cars, because to be seen riding a bike might suggest they couldn't afford a car.

By the late 1960s, Americans' obsession with all things mechanical had begun to wane. People became interested in the environment, and many believed that the best way to experience nature was on a bicycle, not in an automobile. By the 1970s, it wasn't only young people who pedaled around town; adults by the score were leaving their autos at home and purposefully riding their bikes. They rode them to work, for fun, for exercise, to be with their children, to get outdoors—whenever and wherever they could.

This trend continues today. In fact, the United States Cycling Federation (USCF) reports that in 1980 there were 9,089 USCF members. By the year 2000, membership had grown to over 31,000 men, women, and children, representing all 50 states. No wonder the interest in competitive cycling escalates with each Olympic Games —people of all ages are taking a keen interest in Olympic cycling and are rooting enthusiastically for their favorite teams.

Photo courtesy of USOC

The fastest cyclists ride in the lowest, inside lane.

Amateur Cycling Opportunities

Youth

The Lance Armstrong Junior Olympic Race Series for 9-to-18-year-olds is designed to increase awareness of cycling and to increase racing opportunities for junior cyclists. In 1999, 46 races were held throughout the United States, with over 1,500 athletes competing.

Collegians

The National Collegiate Cycling Association (NCCA) program was developed to meet a growing need for a competitive outlet for students at the collegiate level. One of its greatest successes has been the number of women introduced to the sport: more women participate in NCCA activities than in any other significant U.S. cycling program. The NCCA supports three divisions—road, track, and mountain biking—and invites teams assembled through a school's recreation sports or club department to compete. Currently 215 schools are members, more than 2,500 riders are licensed, and approximately 140 events receive permits each year.

Men and Women

The Fresca Men's Amateur Point Series was developed to identify elite talent for the U.S. national team and to improve the quality of racing, by providing amateur riders with a highly competitive series of events.

The Fresca Cup Women's Cycling Series provides highly competitive racing opportunities for women and encourages new cyclists to compete.

Masters (Over 30)

With more than half of USCF members in the masters category of riders who have reached the age of 30, the USCF has established a number of programs for this group. Masters clinics, which are organized by the USCF's regional road and track coaches, are comprehensive. They instruct athletes on evaluating their individual fitness levels, power output, and endurance; identifying their strengths and weaknesses; and formulating personalized training programs. Masters Regional Championships are held in each USCF region, attracting more than 1,900 entries for road events and more than 700 for track events.

Riders with Disabilities

USCF has hosted events for people with disabilities since 1989, and the organization serves as a resource for identifying programs that include athletes with disabilities. USCF's Masters and National Championship programs involve Disabled Sports USA, the United States Association for Blind Athletes, and the U.S. Cerebral Palsy Athletic Association. USCF also publishes a column for cyclists with disabilities in its monthly newsletter *Cycling USA*.

4

USA Cycling

USA Cycling is the national governing body for amateur and competitive cycling in the United States, a member of the U.S. Olympic Committee, and recognized by the International Cycling Union as the sole sanctioning body for cycling in the United States. USA Cycling is the corporate umbrella for the United States Cycling Federation (USCF) for road and track racing; the National Off-Road Bicycle Association (NORBA) for mountain bike racing; the United States Professional Racing Organization (USPRO) for professional road racing; and the National Bicycle League (NBL) for bicycle moto-cross (BMX) racing. All these associations share resources for the common success of the sport.

Headquartered at the U.S. Olympic Training Center in Colorado Springs, CO (with another office in Columbus, OH, for the NBL), USA Cycling maintains a significant presence on the local level through its more than 90,000 members and more than 2,000 clubs in all 50 states, the District of Columbia, and Puerto Rico. During 1998, USA Cycling issued nearly 5,000 permits for events; another 1,795 permits were issued in 1999.

The organization also maintains a significant presence on national and international levels through the development and maintenance of national teams to compete in world championships and the Olympic Games.

USA Cycling is one of the few national governing bodies that has been able to keep, and even increase, corporate sponsorship and revenue during non-Olympic years. The organization has been especially fortunate in developing a close relationship with EDS, which supports USA Cycling in the areas of information and technology management, systems development, business planning, creative and promotional work, and U.S. National Team operations.

Programs and Events

As part of its mission, USA Cycling sponsors many educational programs and events throughout the year. They include coaching clinics, NORBA junior development camps, collegiate cycling camps, national and regional results and ranking systems, a Junior Olympic Mountain Bike Series, local BMX track development, the Marty Nothstein Junior Olympic Series (track), and the Lance Armstrong Junior Olympic Racing Series (road). Their event properties include:

- American Mountain Bike Challenge Series
- EDS Track Cup
- Chevy Trucks/NORBA Championship Series
- Saturn USPRO Cycling Tour
- Collegiate National Championships
- USPRO National Criterium
- USCF Cyclo-Cross National Championships
- USCF Masters National Championships
- EDS National Track Cycling Championships
- NBL BMX National Championship Series
- USCF Elite Road National Championships
- ESPN television productions

- Hosting mountain bike and track World Cup events
- Mercury Tour
- USCF Junior National Championships
- NBL Grand Nationals

There are also new initiatives from USA Cycling. The USA Cycling Development Foundation (USACDF) is the nonprofit fund-raising arm of cycling for U.S. national and Olympic team young-athlete development. The Foundation receives no federal funding or subsidies and operates solely through private donations from individuals, corporations, and other foundations.

Project Triad is a plan to use better information to improve athlete performance, and Kids on Bikes is a program to introduce children to bicycle racing. Finally, there is the National Results and Rankings System.

USA Cycling is a one-stop resource for information about U.S. cycling races, teams, clubs, and programs. For a complete set of rules or more information, contact USA Cycling.

USA Cycling
One Olympic Plaza
Colorado Springs, CO 80909

Tel: (719) 578-4581   Fax: (719) 578-4596

Online: www.usacycling.org

E-mail: usac@usacycling.org

Cycling Rules

USA Cycling has specific age groups and racing ages for its members. Your racing age is defined as your age on December 31 of the current year. The ages and groups (categories) are:

Racing	Age Group
Under 10	Youth
10-18	Junior
19-22	Espoir
23-29	Elite
30+	Master

At cycling races, riders race in the category (age group) stated on their licenses. Elite and Masters riders race in events for their age group or younger. They may not, however, compete in races exclusively for the Espoir group. Espoirs may race in the Elite age group. They may not race in the Masters age group. Women are free to enter any race as long as they meet all eligibility requirements for age, category, and performance.

The U.S. Cycling Federation (USCF) has adopted general rules that apply to any event for which the USCF has issued a permit. A few are summarized here.

- A bicycle race is a race between cyclists on bicycles. Based on performance, awards are given.

- An invitational race is one limited to invited riders.

- A youth race is for riders younger than 10 years old, or up to 15 years old, if there is no junior race for them. The race is held on a closed course.

- A club ride is for training purposes and is for members of USCF-licensed bicycle clubs.

- At least half of a team's riders must be women to make up a mixed team.

- Racing age is the rider's age on December 31 of the current year.

- A sequence of races make up a session. There are no major time breaks.

All participants in racing events are expected to exhibit good conduct. They may be disciplined or even suspended for:

- Theft, fraud, or gross unsportsmanlike conduct

- Using an assumed name

- Trying to fix the results of a race

- Trying to take a short cut during a race

- Showing disrespect to officials, race organizers, riders, or spectators

- Using foul or abusive language or physical abuse

- Interfering with the progress of another rider

- Riding in a dangerous manner

- Pushing or pulling an opponent in any way—clothes, body, or equipment

- Trying to progress without a bicycle

- Causing a crash through negligence

- Being on a race course during an event for which the rider is not entered

- Consuming alcoholic beverages during a race

Types of Track Races

There are several different cycling races, in addition to those discussed earlier in this book. Track racing, for example, includes many types of competitive events.

Scratch Race

All riders in this race start at the same time from the same place. They all start from "scratch." No rider has a starting advantage, and the winner is the rider who crosses the finish line first. If the official race announcement states it specifically, free laps of up to 1,300 meters are allowed if a rider has a mishap. A "mishap" is defined in the *2000 Rulebook* of the USCF as follows:

> A **mishap** is a crash or a mechanical accident (tire puncture or other failure of an essential component). However, a puncture caused by the tire coming off due to inadequate gluing is not a mechanical accident, nor is a malfunction due to misassembly or insufficient tightening of any component. A **recognized mishap** is a stoppage that meets the above conditions. An **unrecognized mishap** is a stoppage where the above conditions are not met. For example: A broken toestrap or cleat is a mishap. A worn or misadjusted cleat or toestrap is not a mishap. If more than one toestrap is used on a pedal, breakage of one is considered a mishap.

Handicap Race

In this race, the stronger riders start later or ride farther. This is done to even out the competition. There is an official handicapper who decides the distance or time for each rider. When two or more riders have the same handicap and start from the same point, safety requires that they be side by side or one after the other.

Miss-and-Out

This is a mass-start race—nicknamed "devil take the hindmost"— with the last cyclist dropping out after any specified period. When a rider must drop out—after every lap, after every other lap, or on some other schedule—is decided before the race, so all riders know the rules. A fast rider can gain a lap if he reaches a point where he is "sheltered" behind the last rider of the group.

The miss-and-out continues until the last person or a set number of riders remains. If several riders remain, there might be a free lap and a sprint to determine the winner.

Sprint

Sprints are a series of track races with a few riders. Sometimes there is a flying start 200-meter time trial to "seed" riders for the sprints. (This information is always available for competitors in the official race announcement.) Sprint races are three laps on a track 333.33 meters or less. If the track is larger, there are two laps. Riders draw lots for their starting positions.

Round-robin Event

This race matches each rider against every other rider, and the winner of each pairing receives one point. When a round-robin event has only a few entrants, the riders may compete with one another two or three times to decide the winner of a pairing.

Tandem Sprint

Tandem sprint races sometimes seed riders using a flying start time trial of 400 meters or the length of the track being used, whichever is less. These sprints are run in the number of laps nearest to 1,500 meters, and no more than four tandems may be raced together on this size track. On tracks smaller than 333 meters, only three tandems may be raced together.

Keirin

This sprint race has the riders complete a set number of laps behind a pacer. Then they sprint. The pacer starts at 25 km/h and increases his speed gradually to 45 km/h. He leaves the track about 600-700 meters before the finish. Racers draw lots for their starting positions, with no more than nine riders in a Keirin. The race itself is 8 laps on a 250-meter track, 6 laps on a 333-meter track, and 5 laps on a 400-meter track.

Time trials differ from sprint races because riders are timed over a fixed distance, and they ride one at a time. Mishaps do occur, and a rider may be allowed a delayed restart if the mishap is verified by the official in charge. Time trials include the following competitive events.

Flying Starts

If a track is 333 meters or less, riders are allowed 2 laps before the actual timing begins. If a track is more than 333 meters, 1 to 1 1/2 laps are allowed.

Standing Start Events

The rider is held, but not pushed or restrained, by an official. The official—the starter—has to be sure each rider starts in the sprinters' lane, with the edge of his front wheel over the starting line, but the wheel must not be pointed up or down the track.

Kilometer Time Trial

The competitors race two at a time—one on each side of the track—using the same starting procedures as in the individual pursuit.

Individual Pursuit

In this race, competitors start at equal intervals around the track. The race is run until one rider catches the others or until a distance that was specified in advance is covered. To "catch a rider" means to overtake and draw even.

Championship Individual Pursuit

This race pits two riders against one another. They start on opposite sides of the track, and the pursuit ends when one rider catches the other, or a specified distance is covered. Distances are 3,000 meters for senior women and juniors and 4,000 meters for men.

Each event may have qualifying rounds, quarterfinals, semifinals, and finals. In a finals championship, for example, there are separate lap cards and a bell for each rider. A red disc and a green disc are placed in the homestraight and backstraight, respectively, at the exact starting point of each rider. One green flag and one red flag mark the first kilometer of each rider, respectively. A double green flag and a double red flag mark the last kilometer of each rider.

The two riders take up their positions on the inside of the track, exactly opposite each other. When championship finals begin, the race is started with a gunshot. As in standing-start events, the riders are held, but not pushed or restrained, by officials. Referees determine that all riders begin in the same way: The front part of the front wheel is directly over the starting line, but the bicycle must not be pointed up or down the track. The referee then puts up a flag to indicate that the rider is ready.

Team Pursuit

Team pursuit races are for teams of two or more riders. Rules of the race are announced in advance explaining how many riders must finish the race. The finisher on whom the time is taken must also be announced in advance.

Italian Pursuit

This is a pursuit race over a set distance by teams with any number of riders. The teams start at spaced, equal intervals around the track. The lead rider for each team leads for one or two laps (whichever was specified), then pulls off. The second rider then takes the lead for one or two laps and pulls off. This riding and pulling off continues until one rider per team remains for the last one or two laps. The team with its last rider farthest ahead, when compared to the team's starting position, wins.

Championship Team Pursuit Matches

These races have three or four riders per team and cover 4,000 meters. As many as six riders may be on a team, but no more than four can compete at any session.

Rules similar to the championship individual pursuit regarding the start and the duties of the officials are followed in championship team pursuit matches. An exception is that red and green flags do not mark the first and last kilometer.

These matches do have qualifying, quarterfinal, semifinal, and final rounds. In the qualifying, if one team catches the other, the faster team continues and records a time for the distance. The other team is eliminated. The same procedure holds for the quarterfinal round, except the winner earns a place in the semifinals. In the semifinals and finals, when one team catches another, the starter stops the race. Catching another team occurs when the third rider of one team draws even with the third rider of the "caught" or overtaken team.

In all rounds, if one team does not catch the other, then a gunshot is fired when the first team finishes the specified distance. A second shot is fired when the second team finishes the distance. A team finishes when its third rider crosses the line.

Two teams with the same time at the finish will be placed based on the faster lap times nearest the finish, and three riders must complete the distance. Otherwise, the team cannot be classified.

Points Race

This is an event that combines a rolling-start scratch race and sprints for points on certain laps. Usually, the sprints are every five laps, but they are every 2 kilometers for elite championships.

Omnium

The Omnium is a set of races with riders competing for points in each event. Numbers of points may vary from event to event, but in National Championships, points go 7-5-3-2-1, for first through fifth places. Final standings are based on total points earned in all events.

Types of Road Races

Road races are exactly what the name implies—cycling races outdoors on roads. They can be from one place to another with a set beginning and end, a circuit that begins and ends at the same place, an out-and-back, or a combination of the three. Since there are other vehicles using a road, road races are run so no one is inconvenienced unnecessarily, and these races have strict requirements regarding food, repairs, and the rules of the road.

- Bottles of water or other liquids may be carried, but not in glass containers. Anything thrown away during the ride must be biodegradable.

- Sharing food or liquids is allowed, or receiving them from a bystander, but nothing may be received from a moving vehicle.

- Team members may exchange tires, tools, pumps, wheels, and bicycles.

- Riders must know the rules of the road and obey all traffic regulations. No closed roads, including railroad crossings, are used.

- Riders cannot receive help from riders in a different race or from any motor vehicle.

Individual Road Race

Individual road events are mass-start races of a minimum of 5 kilometers per lap, if ridden on a circuit course. They may also be handicap races, so all riders have a chance to win. A caravan of several vehicles, with officials, observes the race, writes down any rules that are broken, and assists riders in need of help. Officials also follow all the customary rules of the road. Riders receive food and drink at feed zones or during the race. No support vehicles may provide food or drink when a cyclist is climbing or descending a hill or on dangerous curves.

Criterium

This is a race held on a small course, and there is no other traffic—only cyclists. Courses are 800 meters to 5 kilometers and have official repair pits that must be used by the riders. Criterium races may include "primes"—a sprint within the race. Primes may be announced in advance for certain laps, or they may be announced unexpectedly.

Individual Time Trial

This race is against the clock on a circuit or out-and-back course. (A one-way course cannot be used for timing records.) Some of the same rules for indoor racing events apply to an individual time trial road race, e.g., starting at equal intervals, and no pushing or restraining by the officials.

Team Time Trial

Teams of two or more riders compete using road bicycles on an out-and-back, circuit, or one-way course. For timing purposes, only an out-and-back course is used. Ideally, closed roads, or roads with light traffic, are used for these races. A flat course with a wide turnaround point is desirable. Again, only team members may share food, drink, wheels, or bicycles, or help with repairs.

Cyclocross

This can be an endurance race, since it is ridden over rugged ground—no more than 50 percent can be paved—that has obstacles to overcome. The obstacles are man-made and cannot be higher than 40 centimeters. The idea is to have the cyclist complete some of the course on foot. Along the route, there are stations and pits where riders can exchange equipment or bicycles.

Racing Officials

All officials at races are licensed by the USCF, wear the same uniform at races, and perform these duties:

Chief Referee

The chief referee has general supervision of a race. He interprets and enforces USCF rules, including penalties.

Assistant Referees

The assistant referees advise the chief referee, see if any rules are broken, and inspect bicycles before the race.

Starter

The starter calls the riders to the start area and tells them the ride's distance, finish line, and any special rules. He checks to be sure that riders are dressed appropriately, with their racing numbers in the proper location. Riders with nonconforming uniforms or equipment will not be allowed to start.

Scorers

Scorers track the number of laps gained or lost by the riders. They tell the chief judge, at the end of the race, which riders gained or lost laps.

Judges

Judges advise the chief judge, who determines the finish order of a race.

Timers

The chief timer resolves any discrepancies in the timings and gives them to the chief referee. Hand and automatic timing are used; the hand timing serves as a backup in case the automatic timer fails.

Registrars

The registrars check that riders in an event have valid racing licenses and valid identification, are qualified, and are actually entered in the race.

NORBA

The National Off-Road Bicycle Association (NORBA) is the national governing body for the continually growing sport of mountain bike racing in the United States. NORBA sanctions racing and touring events throughout the 50 states and promotes the sport internationally. Mountain biking continues its rise in popularity with more than 30,000 member riders, and more than 40,000 newcomers try mountain bike racing every year.

Most significantly, the sport was recently granted status as an Olympic event and made its debut as an officially sanctioned event in Atlanta in 1996. Both men's and women's cross–country races were held. Fifty riders competed in the men's event; 30 riders in the women's. The mountain bike course did not have long climbs, but had short steep climbs, plus single-track, double-track, and open-jeep trails. Millions of mountain bike fans watched on July 30, 1996, when their sport was showcased for the first time as an Olympic event to other enthusiasts.

Information on local mountain biking clubs can be obtained from the NORBA headquarters in Colorado Springs, CO.

Classes

For mountain-bike racers, competing with other racers who are at the same skill level is very important. Riders with better skills and more strength can be discouraging opponents for a beginner, while those with fewer skills can impede a skilled rider's development.

NORBA has adopted a classification system so that you ride with and compete against individuals who are nearly your age and ability level. A rider's age is based on his age on December 31 of the present year. Categories are based on ability and racing expertise.

>   Junior: 18 and under

>   Senior: 19-29

>   Master: 30 and up

Juniors are subdivided into 10 and under; 12 and under; 14 and under; 16 and under; and 18 and under.

Categories
Beginners

This category is for the entry-level rider. There is no pressure, but rather an opportunity to learn the sport while enjoying mountain biking. However, once you place in the top five in five races, you must advance to the next category.

Sport

In this category, your skills have improved, and you have developed strength and stamina. Most mountain bike participants are in the sport class at events. Once you place in the top five in five races you advance to expert.

Expert

This is a very competitive level. Your skills, strength, and stamina are very high. If you place in the top five in three NORBA National Championship Series (NCS) events or UCI World Cup events, you may become a semi-pro (men) or pro (women).

Semi-pro

You have to request this level, which is available through the NORBA office or your regional coordinator. Professional teams look for new talent from this category. It is for men only.

Pro

You have to request this level through NORBA or the competition director. It is for both men and women.

NORBA Competitions

NORBA emphasizes the need for cyclists to use and maintain reliable equipment, and to have an independent spirit that exhibits self-reliance and individuality. The challenge for off-road cyclists is to meet these goals while competing in the nine different NORBA competitions, ranging from cross-country to snow biking. A few NORBA racing regulations are summarized here:

- Riders must attend any pre-race briefing, and they must be officially entered in the race.

- Not knowing the rules is no excuse for breaking them.

- Racers must ride the entire event on the same bicycle they began on.

- Riders must perform their own repairs. No help is allowed.

- Riders must carry their own spare parts and tools. "Cannibalizing" another bicycle is not allowed.

- No shortcuts are permitted. Riders must stay on the marked course.

- Any unsportsmanlike conduct—verbal or physical—is prohibited and punished.

- Public or private property must not be destroyed, and all local laws and ordinances must be obeyed.

- Punishments and/or penalties are determined by the race official or NORBA.

Cross-Country

As the name implies, this is a mass-start or individual competition on a circuit course made up of forest roads, forest or field trails, and unpaved dirt or gravel roads. There are feed zones and water zones, but they must be placed so they don't interfere with other riders. The right-of-way belongs to riders; riders pushing or carrying a bicycle must yield. No rider, of course, may use his body to interfere with any other rider.

Point-to-Point

This competition runs from point A to point B and is a mass-start or individual competition. The course is made up of forest roads, forest or field trails, and unpaved dirt or gravel roads as in cross-country races. The rules and regulations are similar to cross-country.

Hill Climb/Uphill

This is exactly what the name implies: a climb up to the finish line. This competition is timed and may be either a mass start or a time trial.

Downhill

This is a time trial with the finish line lower than the start line. Racers usually start at timed intervals and are able to practice on marked courses for this race.

Dual Slalom

In this event, two competitors race down two nearly identical parallel slalom courses. All racers have at least one practice run down the course.

Stage Races

Stage races are a series of events, such as an uphill, a cross-country, and a downhill time trial, taking place over one or more days. They are individual and team competitions, held under NORBA general rules and regulations, but with one exception—how each stage of the race will be conducted is spelled out in a special *Race Bible.* Each stage must be completed and the times or points recorded. The winner is the rider with the lowest cumulative total time or the highest point total at the end.

Observed Trials

These competitions take place over an obstacle course that is in sections. (The sections can be mud, rocks, water, or natural hazards.) Riders are challenged to negotiate each section without touching the ground with a foot or hand (known as a "dab"). A dab adds one point to the rider's score, and the lowest score wins the event.

Competitors in observed trials are placed in one of three classes and four categories by NORBA.

Classes   *Junior* - Age 18 and under (20-inch wheel minimum)

Stock Bike

Trials/Modified Bike

Categories   *Beginner:* First-time competitor

Sport: Riders with above-average skills in observed trials

Expert: Riders especially skilled at observed trials

Pro: Requires an upgrade

Equipment

A stock bike is an unmodified mountain bike with a 40-inch wheelbase, minimum; a rear derailleur with five or more gears; and a 26-inch front wheel and a 24-inch rear wheel, minimum. (No bikes in need of repair or considered dangerous are allowed to race.)

A trials section for the Beginner to Sport level might include hills with difficult traction, logs of less than 8 inches, or very tight turns on level ground. These sections are good training in the skills needed for observed trials.

A trials/modified bike has 20-inch wheels, minimum; brakes on both wheels; and a pedal crank system. The sections for trials bikes are challenging and may include any number of logs or rocks, even double logs, and combinations of different types of traction.

Ultra Endurance Racing

Ultra evidence events are for the most fit riders and cover more than 75 miles or 12 hours. They are longer than cross-country events.

Snow Biking

This is an off-road biking event held on snow. It follows all NORBA rules and regulations and has both Alpine and Nordic events.

Alpine Events	**Nordic Events**
Downhill	Cross-Country
Super Giant Slalom	Point-to-Point
Giant Slalom	Criterium or Circuit
Dual Slalom	
Biker Cross	

International Course Markings

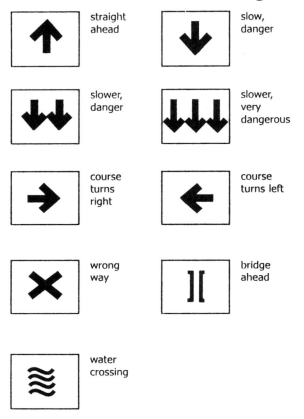

The NORBA Code

As stated in the *2000 NORBA Rulebook*, and reprinted with NORBA's permission, all riders are expected to follow this code:

1. I will yield the right of way to other non-motorized recreationists.

2. I will use caution when overtaking another and will make my presence known well in advance.

3. I will maintain control of my speed at all times.

4. I will stay on designated trails.

5. I will not disturb wildlife or livestock.

6. I will not litter.

7. I will respect public and private property.

8. I will always be self-sufficient.

9. I will not travel solo when bikepacking remote areas.

10. I will observe the practice of minimum impact bicycling.

11. I will always wear a helmet whenever I ride.

5

Buying a Bicycle

There are several points to consider before buying a bicycle. Two of the most important are (1) the type of cycling you want to do, and (2) the amount of money you can afford to spend. If your goal is simply to take leisurely rides around your neighborhood, you can probably find a suitable bike for a modest amount of money. In fact, a used bike in good condition may be just what you're looking for. On the other hand, if you are serious about long-distance or competitive cycling, a bicycle of that caliber will cost quite a bit more.

If you are not yet sure of your goals, consider buying a modestly priced all-purpose bicycle to get started. Take it on short rides and long rides; if you can find them, try some smooth off-road trails. See which you most enjoy, then purchase a good bike especially suited to that purpose. The advantage of this approach is that you don't spend a great deal of money for, say, a touring bike, only to discover that what you really enjoy is off-roading.

Bike Shops

There are many advantages to purchasing a bicycle from a reputable bike shop. Most have well-trained, knowledgeable personnel who will answer your questions and spend the time to make sure you get a bicycle that fits you properly and meets your needs. If you do not feel that you are getting good service at a particular shop, try another one. Bicycles are expensive; don't buy anything until you are satisfied and your questions have been answered.

When you are ready to move up to a more sophisticated bike, you may be able to trade in your old bike and apply its value to the purchase price of a new one. Bike shops are more inclined to work a fair deal with you if you purchased your old bike from that store.

If you decide to become a competitive racer moving up the cycling categories, then you should consult the latest edition of USA Cycling's rule book for specific equipment requirements.

Full-service bike shops have repair technicians on hand who are familiar with the bikes sold in that shop and can give your bike the very best care. Also, a professional bicycle technician has access to the proper parts—both for repairs and for upgrades—and can give you sound advice about these matters. Listen carefully to his or her recommendations.

When you purchase a bike at a bike shop, you will be given a "bill of sale" showing that you lawfully purchased the bike and that you are the legal owner. In the event your bike is stolen, your bill of sale from the bike shop lets the police know that you are indeed the rightful owner. A note of caution is in order here: If you purchase a bike from a private party and the bike was stolen to begin with, that person does not have the legal right to issue you a bill of sale. Bicycle thieves cannot legally transfer ownership. Moreover, if you claim ownership of such a bike, you can be liable for accepting stolen property! You can avoid this aggravation by purchasing your bike from a legitimate, professionally operated bicycle shop.

BMX Bikes

One style of bike that is especially popular with young riders is the BMX. This small, sturdy bike gets its name from cross-country motorcycle racing. Motorcycle racing that takes place on a purpose-built track is called "motocross," abbreviated "MX." Enthusiastic young bicyclists first tried to imitate their motorcycle-riding heroes by putting their street bikes through the same leaps, spins, and jumps. Needless to say, the street bikes fell apart. Bicycle manufacturers quickly saw the need for small, lightweight—but very sturdy—bikes that could withstand the stress of imitation motocross stunts. Hence, the BMX evolved. The name BMX, therefore, is a cross between "B" for bicycle and "MX" for motocross. Nowadays, there are many manufacturers, both in Europe and in North America, who produce strong, well-built BMX bikes.

When purchasing a BMX bike, keep the following points in mind:

- BMX bikes are not made with the variety of frame sizes available in other types of bikes. The most popular frame sizes are 12- and 16-inch, but a few manufacturers now make a 20-inch frame to fit older/taller BMX enthusiasts.

- You fit a BMX to your body by raising or lowering the seat. Stand next to the bike in your stocking feet. Keep your feet together. When the seat post is bolted in its mid-position, the top of the bicycle seat should be even with your seat. If the seat post is all the way up or down, try another bike. There are two reasons for this: (1) the seat post is at its weakest when in an extreme position, and (2) you have nowhere to go with the seat if you experience a growth spurt.

- Since BMX bikes have only one gear, you do not have to worry about fitting your hands to shift controls. But you do have to make sure the handlebars are comfortable and properly adjusted. Your bike shop can help you with these and other adjustments.

Mountain Bikes

The mountain bike is much more than a "big brother" of the BMX. Although both are well-suited to off-road cycling, the mountain bike gives the rider a choice of gears, and the larger frame, wheelbase, and tires give the mountain bike exceptional versatility.

The most important part of a mountain bike is the frame. Yes, this can be said for all styles of bikes, but mountain bikes really take a beating going cross-country, and cyclists often ride miles from civilization. You simply do not want to have major mechanical breakdowns out on the trail. As discussed earlier, BMX bikes certainly get a workout, but cyclists are usually either on a purpose-built track or relatively close to home. If BMX bikes need a major repair, the riders don't have far to walk. Not so with mountain bike enthusiasts—they have been known to ride 50 miles or more into the woods.

A strong, well-built, and well-maintained machine is especially important to mountain bike racers who, according to competition rules, must be self-sufficient and make their own repairs. For your own safety, learn basic maintenance before venturing too far afield.

This competition mountain bike has shock-absorbing forks.

When purchasing a mountain bike, keep the following points in mind:

- The *reach*—the distance from the seat to the handlebars—is paramount for comfortable mountain biking. This is not an idle luxury, but a vital part of mountain bike safety. When descending hills or climbing in loose gravel or sand, you'll want to shift your weight over your rear tire while keeping a firm, steady grip on the handlebars. You can't do either effectively if the reach is incorrect. The length of the top tube relative to your body proportions is a very important consideration.

- Do not get a bike that is too big for you. It is a common misconception that one is always better off on a "bigger" machine. Actually, you are in jeopardy on a machine that is too big to handle safely and effectively. Sit on the seat in your stocking feet. Place your heels, not your toes, on the pedals and rotate them backward. If you cannot keep your heels in contact with the pedals without rocking from side to side, you need to lower the seat. If that doesn't do it, get a smaller bike. This one is too big for you.

For easier mounting and dismounting, some cyclists may prefer
the dropped tube model.

- Once you have selected a machine, ask the bike shop technician about handlebar extensions. Most mountain bikes come with relatively straight handlebars that are fine for short rides. For competitive or long-distance biking, however, you may find that the curved ones give you added comfort and control.

Cruisers

The simplest of all bikes to operate is the cruiser. With its wide seat and upright handlebars, you really do just sit back and cruise. It is the coaster brake application, however, that makes the cruiser the ultimate easy rider. Push backward on the pedals to stop, push forward on them to go, and sit back and enjoy the ride. If your riding is confined to flat terrain and you don't have to go very far at a stretch, the inexpensive, uncomplicated cruiser may be the bike for you. The heavy frame can take a fair amount of bumps and bangs without noticeable damage, and the cruiser adapts very well to accessories such as baskets, book racks, and saddlebags. One reason is that there is almost nothing—gear shift levers, shock-absorbing forks—with which these items could interfere.

Another benefit of the cruiser is its hardiness. If the thought of bicycle maintenance gives you the shivers, a cruiser is your best bet. As long as you have a clean, dry place to store your bike, a general cleaning and a semiannual oiling are about all the maintenance a cruiser requires. Put air in the tires once in a while and you're in business.

The 3-Speed

The 3-speed is much lighter in weight than the cruiser, making it easier to pedal and to steer. Most 3-speeds also have narrower tires than a heavy-framed cruiser, and all multispeed bikes have hand brakes to both wheels.

The 3-speed has a wider seat and upright handlebars.

If you plan to ride more than 5 miles at a stretch and/or if you ride in hilly country, you'll be more comfortable on a multispeed bike.

Most 3-speed bikes have rather wide seats and upright handlebars, similar to those on a cruiser. If you ride in heavily congested areas where speed is not an issue, the upright position makes it easier for you to see obstacles around you. If you plan to do any long-distance riding or if you must traverse steep hills, you may find a 10-speed more comfortable and easier to ride.

The 10-Speed

For many cycling enthusiasts, the ultimate machine is the sleek-as-a-cat 10-speed road racer. Yes, we realize that Tour de France competitors have 16 gears to play with, but we're talking reality here. If you plan to do any racing, long-distance touring, or major hill climbing, you'll need a 10-speed. The large wheels fitted with hard, narrow tires eat up the ground as no other machine can. The turned-down handlebars position you in a more horizontal frame, giving you better wind resistance and allowing you the most efficient means of traveling farther and faster.

If you plan to do any long-distance riding, the seat—professionally known as the saddle—will be of paramount importance. You simply cannot be bothered with an irritating, uncomfortable saddle on a long ride. Racing saddles often are made of titanium, but touring saddles are usually made of plastic or high-quality leather. Some long-distance riders favor plastic because it does not absorb moisture and therefore cannot harbor bacteria; others prefer leather because, being a natural surface, it breathes and conforms slightly to the rider's body. There are many fine saddles on the market, and the choice is entirely yours. Be sure to keep leather saddles out of the rain and occasionally wipe them with saddle soap or leather oil (never machine oil) to keep them soft and pliable.

Bikes with five or more speeds have special gear changers called *derailleurs*. Bikes with derailleurs have one or two gearshift levers. When you move them, the chain moves from one-sized gear to another. A low gear gives the bike the power to climb hills, while a high gear is more efficient on flat, open country.

Whichever bike you choose, give it good care and it will reward you with years of enjoyment.

Turned-down handlebars and large wheels embody the most efficient design for long-distance riding.

6

Clothing and Accessories

Perhaps the two most important considerations when selecting clothing and accessories are safety and comfort. By no means is it necessary to wear the latest fashion or the most expensive brand of apparel, but it is worthwhile to invest in a few items. Clothing especially made for cycling is designed to give you a smoother, more comfortable ride.

Helmets

The most essential piece of equipment you will ever buy is your helmet. For riding in sanctioned events, helmets must conform to specific safety standards. Use these standards as a guideline when selecting a helmet, even for recreational riding. Don't waste your money on a flimsy helmet; get one that meets rigid safety standards. A cycling helmet is an essential piece of equipment for riders of every age and skill level.

Photo by Sandra Applegate

Most employees at top-quality bike shops are very knowledgeable about how cycling helmets should fit. Tell them what type of riding you do and let them guide you in your selection. The three components that make up proper fit are comfort, weight, and ventilation.

First, look for a helmet with good ventilation. Openings along the length are best, with additional holes at the sides. This arrangement will give you the best air flow over your head and will carry excess heat away from your skull.

Once you have found a style with good ventilation, choose the correct size. You can ensure a snug fit by using the additional foam pads that come with most helmets. Once the pads have been inserted, adjust the retention straps. These straps keep the helmet in its proper position on your head.

Photo by Richard Burns

Full-head helmets are an excellent choice for very young children.

Put on the helmet and secure the straps. Now, shake your head from side-to-side. How does it feel? The helmet should feel snug, yet you should have complete flexibility. Tip your head forward and back. If the helmet is too heavy, the weight of trying to balance it all day will severely tire your neck muscles and quickly lead to fatigue.

No matter what else you like about it, never buy a helmet that is too heavy for your body.

Next, can you see clearly? The helmet should not impair your vision. If it comes too far forward on your face, it's probably too big for you. Does the helmet work well with your glasses? Try them both on and shake your head. If the glasses slip out of position, something is wrong. Try repositioning the helmet. If that doesn't solve the problem, it may be that the fit of the glasses is not compatible with the outline of that particular helmet. One or the other will have to go.

Finally, can you hear? No helmet should be so bulky around your ears that you cannot hear clearly. If this is a problem, select another style and repeat the process.

Each of the above steps is important in finding and selecting a properly fitting helmet. No step should be overlooked.

USA Cycling requires that all participants in club rides under a permit from USA Cycling wear a helmet that is securely fastened. This is a mandatory requirement. Failure to wear the proper helmet can result in disqualification from an event and a fine.

Eye Protection

Protective lenses deflect the glare of the sun and protect your eyes from dirt, grit, and other intrusions. For casual or recreational riding, you might think a long-billed cap or colored contact lenses are all the protection you need because they can deflect the sun; however, they can't protect your eyes from debris. Dark glasses are helpful on both counts, but the lenses *must* be made of plastic, not glass. If you have a fall or other mishap and break your glasses, you might have a hard time seeing until

Photo by Sandra Applegate

Some goggles are cool!

they can be repaired. For this reason, the best solution may be goggles. They fit snugly to keep out wind, dust, and other debris; they are made of shatterproof material; and they can deflect the sun on bright days. Moreover, the yellow lenses actually increase illumination on dark, overcast days.

Gloves

Gloves really do help protect your hands, and almost any style of leather or suede gloves is fine for getting started. Gloves with nylon or acrylic palms and fingers should be avoided because they don't provide a secure enough grip on the handlebars or levers. If you really want to be fancy, you can buy a pair of racing gloves, which have gel pads in the palms to improve shock absorption. The casual or recreational rider may not need or want such elaborate accessories. Also, cycling gloves are cut off at the knuckle, thereby exposing your fingers. You may find that regular gloves are more comfortable for you.

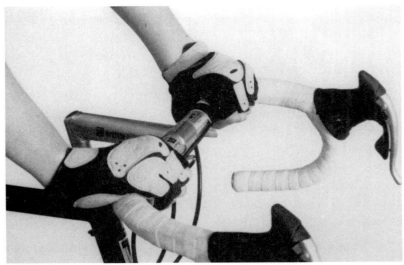

Photo by Sandra Applegate

Cycling gloves have mesh backs for comfort.

Shoes

Although it is not necessary to buy all the bells and whistles for recreational riding, a good pair of cycling shoes is an investment in safety. Sneakers and other types of athletic shoes are too soft for cycling, and many jogging-type shoes are too wide to fit comfortably and safely on the pedals, especially if you are using toe clips or the newer clipless-pedal system. When selecting cycling footwear, keep in mind that you'll need a stiff sole with an upper shoe that will not be adversely affected by scuffs on rocks or branches. For more advanced riding you will probably want to use pedals with toe clips. Cycling shoes are designed to fit neatly into the toe clips; running shoes are too bulky and can actually be dangerous.

Socks should always be worn when cycling. They protect your feet from friction and convey perspiration away from your skin. Natural-fiber materials work best; nylon and other synthetic fabrics do not absorb moisture nearly as well. Whichever type of socks you prefer, wear them when trying on shoes.

Coordinating your socks and shoes will help ensure the best fit, and your best performance as a cyclist.

Shorts and Jerseys

You can increase your comfort by wearing well-fitting cycling shorts. This is not a fashion statement. Cycling shorts are cut to make riding as comfortable as possible—this means no bulky inseam to chafe and irritate your inner thighs. Moreover, cycling shorts are cut extra long in the leg, low in front to make breathing easier, and high in back to keep your lower back warm and covered as you lean forward. For added flexibility, most have either an elastic or a drawstring waist.

For casual riding, a regular T-shirt is fine, but for long-distance rides (and certainly for competitive rides), a cycling jersey is what you need. Cycling jerseys are cut long to keep your lower back covered, yet they gently hug your torso to reduce wind resistance. Any cotton or cotton-blend shirt will do nicely for casual riding. But avoid synthetic fabrics that neither breathe nor absorb moisture—these fabrics are not suitable for sports. You will be more comfortable in natural fiber clothing.

Additional regulations regarding advertising and uniform colors apply for USA Cycling events. At the beginning of all events, of course, riders should present themselves in clean uniforms, including shoes and helmets, that are in good condition. Uniforms may not be torn or in need of repair.

Cold and Wet Weather Attire

Not all cycling is done in warm weather. If you find yourself riding on a damp, windy, or otherwise cold day, a lightweight sweatsuit or jogging suit will be a welcome addition. Make sure your pants legs are snug enough to stay out of the bicycle's moving parts. If necessary, use a pants clip or wrap masking tape around your ankles, putting the excess material on the *outside*. One word of caution: if your sweatshirt has a drawstring neck or a hood, make sure the string is not so long that it can become tangled in the handlebars or levers. For the same reason, scarves and mufflers are not recommended for cycling; it's too easy for them to unwind and get caught in the machinery.

There are specialty items for wet-weather riding, and competition riders use many of these products with great success. Most beginners will be riding in one general locale, so they will not need the variety of materials used by international racers. If you like the idea of wet-weather riding, ask your local bike shop to recommend clothing suitable for your geographic area. There are many differences in the clothing available, and you'll want to get something conducive to the weather (temperature, humidity, wind-chill factor, etc.) in your area.

If you live in an area with terribly cold winters, you may want to postpone cycling until the warmer months. But if you choose to ride in the cold, follow a few safety tips. If the temperature reaches 32 degrees Fahrenheit or below, cover your face. Riding at 20 mph, your flesh can freeze within minutes—and you may not even know it has happened until it's too late.

Wear a wool or wool-blend ski mask or balaclava. Wear plastic, not metal, goggles—metal can freeze to your face! Wear full gloves, preferably insulated ones; and keep your body warm. Do not let perspiration build up on your body. If it does, you could freeze. Ask an experienced cyclist how to dress for cold-weather riding, then follow his or her advice. And finally, if you feel apprehensive about the weather, don't ride. Save it for another day.

In USA Cycling events, nothing may be worn under or over a rider's uniform for the purpose of reducing wind resistance. Rainy weather is the exception. Then, a cover that is meant to keep you dry (or warm in cold weather) is allowed. Shoe covers are allowed in all weather conditions.

Bike Bags

Whether you're commuting to work or heading out for a picnic in the park, the time will come when you'll want to carry papers or belongings with you on your ride.

There are many fine bike bags on the market, ranging widely in size, material, and price. Pick one you like. The important point is to select a true bike bag; i.e., a bag specifically made to be attached to a bicycle. Tying your gym bag or lunch sack to the handlebars is very hazardous. These items can shift while you are riding, get caught in the spokes or stuck under the handlebars, and make it impossible to control the bike. This situation is very perilous if you are riding in traffic.

There are two basic styles to choose from: *panniers*, which fit like saddlebags on a horse, and bags which attach to the handlebars or seat. Go to your local bike shop and select a bike bag large enough to meet your needs.

If you get a bag that is too small, you'll soon have loose items sticking out the top. This is not good. Get one full-sized bag, or two smaller saddlebags, depending on your needs.

Some of the newer bags have map holders, insulated compartments for food and extra water bottles, internal stiffeners to keep a soft item from being crushed, and detachable shoulder straps so you can carry the bag with you when you're off the bike.

A third option is a one-wheeled trailer that attaches to the seat post of your bike and holds up to 75 pounds of your gear. This can be used in the city, or countryside, or out on a trail. But whichever type you select, remember that it is an investment in safety. Select one that fits your needs, your bike, and your price range. You'll be glad you did.

7

Cycling Safety Tips

When we think of recreational cycling, we may visualize ourselves pedaling at a leisurely pace down a quiet country lane, gazing at the trees and flowers along the way. Unfortunately, for an ever-increasing number of cyclists, especially urban dwellers, that scene is simply not a reality. In many parts of the country, the only place cyclists have to ride is on crowded city streets—and that takes special cycling skills.

Riding in Traffic

Do not antagonize drivers of motor vehicles. Even if you believe that you are correct and the driver of the car or truck is in error, your first concern should be for your safety—not your rights. A car or truck is much bigger, heavier, and stronger than your bike. Never argue. Let motorists go first or go around you, whatever they want to do. Keep yourself safe.

You can do a lot to ensure your safety by riding in a predictable manner. Motorists will feel more comfortable if they see you riding smoothly in a calm, controlled manner. Swerving and weaving your bike along the roadway is confusing to drivers and may cause them to make an erratic move themselves.

Remember, a car is bigger than you are—don't force the issue.

Use hand signals to indicate a change of direction. Motorists will have a better chance of staying out of your way if they know which direction you intend to travel.

Look for streets that have a wide shoulder and avoid the busiest streets whenever you can. If possible, adjust your riding schedule so that you are off the street during the heaviest periods of traffic, usually early in the mornings and evenings.

Photo by Sandra Applegate

This businessman commutes in city traffic.

Wear brightly colored clothes during the day and, if you must ride after dark, wear a white jacket or sweatshirt. At night, white shows up better than any other color. Apply strips of reflector tape to your shoes, pants, and jacket. Make sure your bike has a good reflector; apply strips of reflector tape to your bike as well. Reflector ankle straps serve a dual purpose, since they also keep your pants cuffs clean and out of the bike's chain.

Ride in the same direction as the traffic and stay as far to the right as you can. Watch for potholes, drainage ditches, manhole covers, and other urban hazards. In a pinch, ditch to the right; do not turn out into the flow of traffic unexpectedly.

In congested areas, avoid riding side by side with another cyclist. This is very irritating to motorists and may cause them to behave irrationally. Two bikes are difficult for a motorist to pass. The driver may squeeze you and the other cyclists together, causing an accident. For everyone's safety, avoid riding two-or-more abreast on busy city streets.

If you use your bike to carry books, groceries, laundry, sporting equipment, or any other items, make sure the load is well balanced and secured. A load of heavy books, for example, can shift without warning, causing you to lose control of the handlebars. You can help ensure your safety by checking that all loads, no matter how small or how light, are well secured. On windy days, make sure nothing can blow off your bike or out of your basket. Swirling papers or an airborne jacket can be very startling to passing motorists.

At busy intersections, you may be safer by dismounting and walking your bike across the street. Experienced cyclists may prefer to ride across with the traffic, but children and beginners should stop and walk. Once you are on foot, follow crossing directions given for pedestrians, not vehicles.

Never assume a motorist sees you or your bike; defensive cycling is your best protection. At all times, be aware of what vehicles around you are doing, and be prepared to react in any emergency.

Cyclists and the drivers of motor vehicles share public streets, and both have the same rights and responsibilities. Cyclists must obey traffic lights, stop at stop signs, and heed other laws, such as riding single file in their lane and giving hand signals when turning. Remember that in any dispute with the operator of a motor vehicle over the right-of-way, you are the vulnerable one. Yield, even if you are right.

Road Hazards

Even if you don't ride in traffic or other congested areas, you can still encounter various types of road hazards. In this section, we'll take a look at common hazards that a cyclist may encounter, even on a quiet country lane.

Be alert for dogs. Even the most placid dog can be startled by the sight and sound of a passing bicycle. If you are chased by a dog coming from its own yard, try to sprint past the property. Most dogs won't continue to chase you once you are away from their "territory." If that doesn't work, try using your voice sharply, saying "No!" or "Get back!" If you have a water bottle handy, you might try to squirt just enough water to startle the dog, allowing yourself time to make an escape. On no account should you try to provoke a dog, nor should you try to retaliate if you are chased. Leave the dog alone and get on up the road. Of course, if you are bitten, call the police immediately. Give a good description of the dog and the location of the attack. You may ask bystanders if they know where the dog lives, but leave any encounters with the owner to the police.

Natural hazards you may encounter include wind, rain, fog, snow, ice, mud, and sand. Wind can be hazardous for a number of reasons. A strong wind, especially a crosswind, can make it difficult to control your bike. Keep both hands on the handlebars at all times and try to maintain a smooth, steady pace. Blowing sand and dust can get into your eyes, obstructing your vision. If possible, get to a safe shelter and wait for the wind to ease before continuing.

If you get caught out in the rain, slow down, take a steady grip on both handlebars, and ride toward your destination using a route familiar to you. On a wet surface, your bike will require a much longer stopping distance, so brake gently and allow plenty of room. Also, tires are likely to slip on a wet surface. A slow, steady pace and gentle braking will give you the best traction.

Fog is especially hazardous for motorists. The best plan is not to ride in fog. If you must, rely on your hearing as well as your vision to alert you to approaching traffic. Do not assume a motorist sees you. Pull way off the road and wait for any vehicles to pass.

Snow and ice can be very treacherous. Novice cyclists of any age would do well to call for someone to pick them up. Leave winter-weather riding to experienced cyclists.

Mud and sand can surprise you. The road or trail may look perfectly smooth, until suddenly your front tire is sinking like a stone. Don't panic. Take a firm hold on your handlebars, but avoid the "death grip." This is important because if you do fall, you don't want to pull the bike over into your face. Gently shift your weight rearward to distribute more of it over the rear tire. Get your feet down and walk your bike out of the bog.

When riding on pavement, keep an eye out for oil slicks. These can be very treacherous. Ride around oil slicks whenever possible, but check for traffic first. If you can't ride around an oil slick safely, get off and walk.

Potholes, railroad crossings, cattle guards, and drainage grates are all snares waiting to ambush the inattentive cyclist. Railroad tracks, cattle guards, and drainage grates should be crossed at a bit of an angle. This approach keeps your front tire from getting stuck in the cracks. Avoid potholes, especially those filled with water. You can't tell how deep they really are. Heavy jolts are very hard on your bike's suspension. Whenever possible, ride around potholes. Why beat up your bike when you don't have to?

Climbing and descending hills can be loads of fun on a bike, but be aware that your rear tire may slip, especially if you hit loose sand or gravel. When traversing hills, you may want to use a lower gear or try shifting your weight backward over your rear tire. Both techniques will help you gain better traction.

Sharing Roads and Trails

If you see horseback riders approaching, stop and allow them to pass you. Let them get several yards away before you continue. If you come up behind horseback riders, softly call out and request permission to pass. This gives the riders time to get their horses under control. Meeting horses on the road or the trail is a situation where you really have to use common sense and courtesy. Even if you have the technical right-of-way, it is much easier for you to control your bike than it is for a rider to control a live horse. Realize that horses can become easily frightened by a bicycle. Use your head. Yield the right-of-way to horses, and everyone will get where they are going—safely and happily.

Although we do not usually think of horseback riders and joggers as "road hazards"—after all, we all have the right to use the trails—certain conditions involving horses and joggers can be hazardous if not handled properly. If you encounter a jogger, do not assume the person heard you coming and will move out of "your" way. You don't own the road. Pass joggers and hikers carefully and always leave plenty of room. Joggers, especially, may be very tired, and having to dodge your bike could cause them to stumble and fall. Again, common sense and courtesy represent the best approach.

8

Family Cycling

Two styles of bicycles that are popular for family outings are the tandem and the trailer. The graceful bicycle built-for-two was first popular in the 1890s, more than 100 years ago. In fact, the tandem may be one of the few bicycle styles that has ever had a song written about it. At the height of the Gay Nineties, song writer Harry Dacre proclaimed his love for his sweetheart in the popular ballad "Daisy Bell," in which the lyrics note how she'll "look sweet upon the seat of a bicycle built for two!"

Today, tandems are more popular than ever. The Tandem Club of America has 2,500 members and holds rallies where it is not unusual to have 300 teams participate. In fact, since the mid-1980s, the two types of bicycles that have gained most in popularity are the tandem and the mountain bike. Also gaining in popularity is the trailer, especially when fitted with a child's seat.

Tandems

What is it like to ride a tandem? First, tandems require good teamwork and good communication between the two riders. The person in front is called the "captain," and the person in back is called the "stoker." The origins of these terms have been lost through the years, but they are very appropriate. The captain has control of his or her ship, while the stoker's main job is to provide power to the pedals. There are many benefits that go

Courtesy of Tandem Club of America

**This modern tandem is outfitted with three water bottles
for a long-distance ride.**

with being a stoker—he can read maps, give turn signals, and act as a traffic spotter for the captain. Moreover, while the captain is busy watching the road, the stoker can look around and view the scenery. Tandems offer fresh air and exercise, and are a low-cost leisure activity once the bike is purchased. If you aren't riding a tandem, they are certainly graceful to watch from the sidelines.

Tandems come in a variety of prices, sizes, and styles. For casual riding, you may prefer a mountain bike tandem with straight handlebars and an upright riding position. For long-distance touring, you may prefer a racing tandem, complete with downturned handlebars, narrower saddles, and more aerodynamic riding positions. There is even a tandem that travels with you. It can be taken apart and packed in its own carrying case.

Tandems are far more adaptable than people realize. For example, you can outfit most tandems with a youth seat and raised pedals so that an older child can ride safely, yet have a parent or other adult in the captain's seat to do the steering and braking.

If you want to try a tandem, go to a bicycle store that specializes in tandems. Many bicycle stores can order a tandem for you, but if the store personnel are not familiar with tandems, they may, unknowingly, recommend the wrong cycle for you, or order one that simply will not fit. If your bicycle store is not familiar with tandems, ask if there are any experienced tandem cyclists in town. Check with local bike clubs as well as community recreation departments.

If you find a tandem specialist, pay careful attention to his or her instructions about how to ride a tandem. There are certain techniques that are different from riding a single, and if you learn to use them effectively, your tandem riding will be safer and more enjoyable. For more information, contact the Tandem Club of America.

Trailers and Sideriders

Another variation on family cycling is the child trailer. The best child trailers have a wide wheelbase for stability, thick tires for traction, and a cushioned seat for shock absorption. The mountain bike is strong, stable, and has good balance and braking, and many cyclists consider it the ideal choice for towing a trailer.

Children of any age should be outfitted with helmets, and reflector tape should be applied to the rear and both sides of the child trailer. On warm days, a net covering protects children from direct sun. On cool, damp, or windy days, a snap-on hood keeps children warm, yet transparent side curtains enable them to see out.

For a child just learning about cycling, a tandem or trailer arrangement provides a safe environment in which to learn how to deal with traffic, rules of the road, and other situations. There is also a siderider—similar to the old-fashioned police sidecar—that can be used instead of a bike trailer. For larger families, parents often ride the tandem, while older children ride in a bike attachment, and the smallest ride in a trailer towed at the end.

Tandem Racing

In case you still think tandems belong only in Victorian novels, bear in mind that some of the fastest, slickest bicycle racing you'll ever see takes place on modern-day racing tandems. For one thing, the extra weight of two riders, plus double the pedal power, translates into serious speed. Many clubs nationwide hold special tandem races, while others allow tandems to participate

Photo courtesy of Tandem Club of America

Successful tandem racing requires split-second timing and communication between the riders.

in all classes. Tandems very often win open events because the extra speed gives them an enormous advantage. The stoker has a built-in drafting partner and for this reason can keep pedaling at full power longer than could most solo cyclists.

Tandem racing requires split-second timing and an almost "sixth sense" level of communication between the two riders. Of course, you and your partner must practice at the recreational level before you tackle a race, but the opportunities for tandem cycling are limited only by your imagination. If you have always wanted to cycle, but did not feel up to doing it alone, perhaps a tandem partner is just what you've been waiting for.

9

Fitness and Health

Recreational cyclists do not need a round-the-clock training regime, but even casual riders will benefit from a sensible, effective exercise and physical fitness program. According to many sports experts, the best way to begin any fitness program is *slowly*. Just as you would not try to ride 500 miles your first day out, your off-the-bike fitness program must build gradually, as well. Take it easy and progress slowly, but steadily. You can't succeed in any sport without getting into and maintaining good health and physical fitness. A major fringe benefit of cycling is that the fitness you develop while learning and training will carry over to any other sports or recreational activities you enjoy—for example, soccer, gymnastics, or swimming.

A proper warm-up is essential, and the cornerstone of your fitness program should be the stretching exercises. Cycling keeps muscles, tendons, and nerves contracted; your arms, legs, and back do not get to operate through their full range of motion. This contracted state is demanding on the body and must be relieved. The best remedy is a total range-of-motion workout—and that means stretching.

Stretching

One way to strengthen and limber your body is to stretch every day, even on the days you do not ride your bike. Do not pull yourself into an exaggerated or painful position—that is not stretching, that is torture. Such extremes will not help you and may even cause an injury. Follow these simple guidelines for effective stretching.

If you are warming up outdoors, stay out of drafts and keep your body warm. A lightweight sweatsuit is ideal, and you can easily put it on over your cycling clothes. After you warm up, keep the suit on until you are ready to ride. Drink fluids to cool and refresh your body, but do not expose yourself to a blast of cold air.

If you are stretching indoors, find a spot with plenty of open space. Your efforts will be pointless if the space you are working in is so cramped you cannot extend yourself. When stretching indoors be mindful of air conditioning. The effect can be as deleterious as any outdoor elements. Keep your body warm and protected.

Once you have found a comfortable place to exercise, clear your mind of any stress and relax. It is hard to get the benefit of your stretching exercises if your mind remains cramped. Your goal is to loosen and limber your body, and it is hard to do that unless your mind is equally relaxed.

Start slowly. Affect an easy stretch and hold that position for 20 to 30 seconds. Release slowly and repeat on the opposite side of your body. For example, if you begin by stretching your left arm, repeat that exercise with the right arm. Stretch and hold both sides of your body for the same length of time.

Never bounce. Years ago, people thought bouncing helped stretch the muscles. Fitness experts now know this is not true. Bouncing is, in fact, counterproductive. It tightens the very muscles and ligaments you are trying to stretch.

Resist any temptation to rush through your exercises. Take your time, breathe slowly and deeply, concentrate on what you are doing. Relax.

It is natural to feel a little tighter or stiffer on some days than on others. Do not force the issue and do not hurt yourself by trying to "work it out." Your body is telling you it is tired—give it a rest. Do a light workout and leave the more difficult moves for another day. Note: If this is a cycling day for you, take a leisurely ride on flat ground. Tackle the hills on a day when you feel more limber.

The following stretches will help you avoid most of the physical problems encountered by cyclists.

Neck Stretch

Illustrations in this chapter courtesy of USA Cycling

Stretch your neck in three steps. First, tilt your head repeatedly from front to back. Then, tilt it from side to side. Finally, rotate it in a circular motion.

Shoulder Stretch

Stretch your arms down to your waist and then behind your head, an arm at a time. Rotate your arm in each position to make sure that all of your shoulder muscles are stretched.

Quadriceps Stretch

While leaning on a solid object, grab your ankle and pull it upward with your arm. Alternate legs.

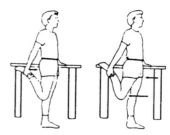

Calf Stretch

With your weight on the front foot, bend your rear knee forward to stretch your calves and your Achilles tendons. Be sure that the toes of the rear foot remain on the ground. Then, alternate legs.

Hamstring Stretch

Perform this stretch by flattening your back and leaning forward. This stretches the extended leg. Alternate legs.

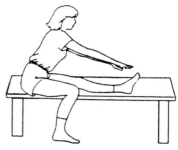

Lower Back Stretch

While lying on your back, alternately pull each knee toward your chest and slowly straighten your leg.

Wrist Stretch

With your fingers pointing toward your knees, lean forward. This stretch helps prevent handlebar palsy.

Remember that regular stretching is the key to success. A light session every day is far more beneficial (and healthier) than one rigorous session once in a blue moon.

Toning and Conditioning

Many cyclists like to augment their bike riding with regular workouts at a gym. One advantage of a good gym or health club is the access it gives you to resistance training (also known as weight training) machines.

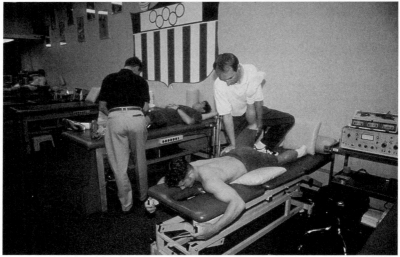

Photo courtesy of USOC

A good rubdown relaxes and tones muscles and ligaments, and is an essential training component for all U.S. Olympic and elite athletes. Many gyms and fitness centers now offer massage therapy. If possible, make massage a part of your overall conditioning program.

Many sports experts who specialize in cycling recommend the use of machines rather than free weights. It is too easy to hurt yourself waving free weights around in all directions. The machines give you a controlled workout. Start with the lowest weight setting and increase the amount of resistance a little at a time. For optimum health and fitness, stretch before and after working on the machines.

Saddle Sores

Frequently, riders develop saddle sores during the conditioning phase of training. The reason is that you are now spending more time on your bike and taking a little more serious approach to your riding. The increase in stress, training, and time in the saddle all contribute to the development of skin rashes, saddle sores, and other discomforts.

The good news is that, if treated immediately, most saddle sores disappear within a few days and do not cause lasting or serious damage. The operative phrase here is "if treated immediately." Never leave a saddle sore, or any other skin irritation, untreated.

The term "saddle sore" is actually a collective term for any skin irritation, pain, or abrasion around your crotch, seat bones, or inner-thigh area. Those parts of your skin that rest on or rub against the bicycle seat are subject to chafing and other problems. Saddle sores are most often caused by one of three factors: friction, pressure, or infection.

Chafing of the inner thighs is a very common friction-induced condition. When the inner thighs repeatedly rub against the sides of the bicycle seat—a condition that occurs during pedaling—the skin becomes raw and irritated. Left untreated, chafing can become very severe. The best approach is to wash and gently dry the legs every day, exposing them to fresh air and as much sunlight as possible. Some people find relief with topical creams and lotions; others like to use dry powder. All of these are fine and largely a matter of choice, but the most important step is good daily hygiene.

Saddle sores are often caused by pressure on the crotch and inner-thigh area. As your training and conditioning increase, you will naturally be spending more time on your bike, riding more miles per session. Pressure can build during long rides, preventing small blood vessels from bringing a full supply of blood to the skin. When the skin gets a less-than-adequate blood supply, saddle sores can quickly develop. If you begin to feel discomfort, get off your bike and walk around for a few minutes. Walking will restore an adequate blood supply to your body, and give cramped muscles and nerves a chance to stretch and open up as well.

As soon as you get home, remove your cycling clothes and get right into a shower or bath. Dry thoroughly and, if possible, wear loose-fitting clothing for the remainder of the day. Unrestrictive clothing will allow your body to get the fresh air it needs. Fresh air to the skin reduces the chance of developing an infection.

Infection can be controlled by keeping yourself and your clothes clean and fresh. For long-distance riding, it is best to wear padded cycling shorts designed to whisk moisture away from your body. Avoid wearing the same shorts two days in a row without first laundering them and letting them dry completely. Worn clothing holds bacteria and increases your chances of developing a skin infection.

If you do not have or cannot afford more than one pair of "real" cycling shorts, that's fine. Simply wear sweatpants or another pair of comfortable shorts, preferably cotton, on alternate days. Jerseys, T-shirts, and socks likewise should be changed daily. A sweaty T-shirt or dirty socks invite bacteria.

Pay special attention to your feet, especially the tender skin between your toes. This is an area where bacteria love to hang out, causing the painful disease commonly known as "athlete's foot." You can usually beat this monster by keeping your feet clean and allowing them to dry thoroughly after every washing, and by wearing clean socks every day. Taking care of your cycling clothes is not about making a fashion statement; it is about protecting your health.

Nutrition

Good eating habits go hand-in-hand with fitness training. You can be in good health without being physically fit, but you can't become physically fit without following a well-balanced diet that contains protein, fats, and carbohydrates in the proper amounts.

Carbohydrates are sugars and starches and come in two forms—simple and complex. The simple form, found in processed foods like candy, soft drinks, or sweet desserts, is the one to avoid. These provide only "empty" calories that may taste good momentarily but do nothing for overall health. This is low-quality nutrition. It's not necessary to eliminate them entirely from your diet, but be selective. (Your dentist will be happy, too.) Sugar, in its natural form, is abundant in fresh fruit, and a better way to satisfy a sweet tooth is by eating a piece of fruit, rather than a candy bar.

Snacking in front of the television seems to be another American dietary habit, but for the athlete who is serious about getting fit, there is no place for high-fat, high-salt, high-calorie "junk food" in the diet. Try munching on an apple, tangerine, or carrot or celery sticks while you watch your favorite show or when you need a snack during the day.

The U.S. Department of Agriculture (USDA) and the Department of Health and Human Services (DHHS) reissued "Dietary Guidelines for Americans" in May 2000. These revised guidelines emphasized the importance of carbohydrates and the lesser role of protein and fats in a healthful nutrition program.

Complex carbohydrates are an athlete's best nutritional friend because they are a primary source of fuel. You'll find them in bread, vegetables of all colors (especially peas and beans), fruit, nuts, pasta, and whole grains (wheat, rice, corn, and oats). They should make up about 60 percent of your well-balanced, nutritious meals throughout the day, starting with the first one.

Protein is found in many foods—nuts, dairy products, and lean meats, poultry, and low-fat fish. You don't need a 16-ounce steak every day to "build muscle." In fact, that's probably too much protein for your body to absorb efficiently; the rest just goes to waste. Try to keep your protein consumption to about 20 percent of what you eat each day, and you'll consume enough to build muscle, maintain it, and repair it when necessary.

A Guide to Daily Food Choices

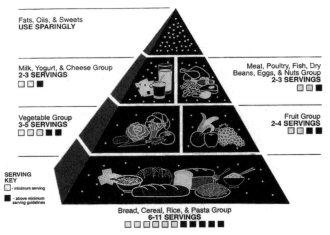

Fats, Oils, & Sweets
USE SPARINGLY

Milk, Yogurt, & Cheese Group
2-3 SERVINGS

Meat, Poultry, Fish, Dry
Beans, Eggs, & Nuts Group
2-3 SERVINGS

Vegetable Group
3-5 SERVINGS

Fruit Group
2-4 SERVINGS

SERVING
KEY
☐ - minimum serving
■ - above minimum serving guidelines

Bread, Cereal, Rice, & Pasta Group
6-11 SERVINGS

Source: U.S. Department of Agriculture and the U.S. Department of Health and Human Services

Your body does need some fat, but not nearly as much as most Americans consume every day from a diet that is often overloaded with fat and salt. The fat you eat should come from margarine, vegetable oil, or nuts and should be no more than 20 percent of your daily intake of food. Fat has some benefits; it is an insulator in cold weather and an energy source. But a little goes a long way to keep an athlete healthy and fit.

Don't skip meals—especially breakfast. Breakfast is like putting gas in your car—you need it to get started—and that meal should be a good solid one-third of your daily calorie intake. Not hungry for breakfast in the morning? Try this once: Eat a light dinner the night before. You'll have an appetite in the morning, and that should help get you on a regular meal schedule. It may be a cliché, but eating breakfast will make you feel better all day. Also, there is no nutritional law that requires a "traditional" breakfast. There is nothing wrong with eating a baked potato, having a hearty soup, or eating lean meat, fish, or poultry at your first meal of the day. The important point to learn is to eat well-balanced, nutritious meals throughout the day, starting with your first one.

A word on liquids: Avoid cola drinks, coffee, and tea. They are loaded with caffeine and act as diuretics to take water from your body. The one liquid you should not avoid is water, which is 60 percent of your body's weight and is needed to lubricate your joints and maintain body temperature. Water is also the transportation system for the nutrients you need to stay healthy, so don't neglect this crucial liquid. One to two quarts per day will keep your body well-lubricated and prevent dehydration. No one's body ever adapts to dehydration, so the cyclist must stay hydrated by drinking water. Do not let yourself become thirsty. If you do, you've waited too long to rehydrate.

The new dietary guidelines suggest that Americans ". . . limit the intake of beverages and foods that are high in added sugars." For example, a Food and Drug Administration (FDA) study, published early in 2000, reported that soda consumption per person in the United States had reached 41 gallons in 1997. This is nearly double the 1970 consumption rate of 22 gallons. A 12-ounce can of soda contains 9 teaspoons of sugar, an amount that you could visualize by measuring this amount into a cup or glass. Container sizes have kept pace with consumption, from the standard 6.5-ounce bottle of the 1950s to today's 12-, 20-, and 64-ounce containers. As soda consumption has gone up, milk, juice, and water consumption has gone down. Unfortunately, the high-calorie drinks don't contain the vitamins and minerals needed for good health.

A recent study at Harvard University of adolescent girls (whose bones are maturing) indicates that many are drinking more sodas, not eating calcium-rich foods, and not getting enough weight-bearing exercise, such as running or tennis. Long range, these dietary deficits can lead to thin, brittle bones that fracture easily.

The problem is of such concern that the DHHS, the Centers for Disease Control (CDC), and the National Osteoporosis Foundation are cooperating in an information campaign aimed at 9- to 12-year-old girls. The campaign emphasizes the importance of calcium in the diet, the foods that are good sources of calcium, and the importance of combining weight-bearing exercise with calcium intake.

The dietary guidelines also make statements about exercise and about sodium (salt) in the diet. For the first time, Americans are urged to include "moderate daily exercise" of at least 30 minutes per day in their lifestyles and to ". . . choose and prepare foods with less salt." This means avoiding soy sauce, ketchup, mustard, pickles, and olives.

Carbohydrate-rich drinks are an effective way of replenishing the nutrients your body needs during vigorous exercise, such as cycling. You can prepare a healthful drink and carry it on your bike in your water bottle. A complex carbohydrate drink prepared by mixing cornstarch with water is very nutritious. The cornstarch is flavorless, and the drink contains no salts or sugars to cause an upset stomach. If you don't want to mix your own, there are many commercially prepared drinks available. By sipping at regular intervals, you can rehydrate and feed your body at the same time.

It is important to fuel your body before you embark on a long ride, but avoid excess fat and any foods difficult to digest. After all, the purpose of your meal is to give you energy, not a stomachache.

While there are no "miracle" foods, by eating a carbohydrate-rich diet the cyclist can improve performance and extend endurance for those long rides. The U.S. Cycling Federation's suggested diet plan is as follows:

- A few days before a ride: Eat 600 grams of carbohydrate per day and drink at least eight glasses of pure water.

- Three hours before a ride: Eat one solid meal that you would normally eat every day.

- Two hours before a ride: Hydrate your body by drinking one liter of water or a sports drink.

- Ten minutes before a ride: Drink one bottle of pure water.

- During your ride: After 15 or 20 minutes, begin drinking a high–carbohydrate sports drink. If this is a long ride of more than three hours, have bagels or other high–carbohydrate foods, and a sports drink with a 5 to 10 percent carbohydrate concentration. Keep in mind that you want to replace the fluids your body will lose while you are riding.

- Experiment with different foods during training, but never during a race.

- Finally, eat before you are hungry, and drink before you are thirsty!

If you have additional questions about good food choices for cyclists, consult your doctor. You may also find helpful information by contacting the sports medicine departments of various universities.

Finally, there are no "miracle foods" or "miracle diets" or "miracle pills" that will keep you in perfect health and physically fit. A well–balanced diet, paired with regular exercise, will help you stay in shape for life.

Physical Fitness and Conditioning

It is never too soon or too late to begin exercising and getting your body into good working order. If you are overweight, get winded easily, or are otherwise out of shape, you may have difficulty participating in cycling. Consult your physician, however, before beginning any fitness program and work only under the supervision of a qualified, knowledgeable coach or trainer.

The Four Parts of Fitness

Physical fitness has four parts: muscle strength, muscle endurance, cardiovascular (heart, lungs, and blood vessels) endurance, and flexibility. Each part depends on the others to maintain physical fitness. Push-ups, for example, build strong muscles through muscle repetition. Muscle endurance aims to work muscles over a period of time without tiring them. Sit-ups are great for this. Muscles need oxygen to function at peak levels, and this is why the heart, lungs, and blood vessels are so important to physical fitness. They sustain working muscles over long periods of cycling activity.

Muscle Strength

Muscle strength can prevent aches and pains, keep the body aligned properly, and prevent injuries. Building this muscle strength requires fast and long exercise. The muscle gets "tired," but this is what builds strength. Muscles should feel a little uncomfortable, but not painful. The goal is all-over muscle strength, since too much strength in one group of muscles can lead to an injury in another group. Strong muscles with low flexibility can lead to muscle pulls, while flexibility with low muscle strength can lead to dislocations.

Whether you use hand-held dumbbells or sophisticated exercise machines, strength-training techniques work the same way: they pit your muscles against resistance. (An athlete using equipment at a gym needs guidance from a fitness trainer.) Strength grows as resistance is increased, a concept called "progressive overload." Repeated stress thickens the fibers that make up muscles by increasing protein buildup. The thicker the muscle fibers, the stronger the muscles.

A strength-training session includes exercises for all the major muscle groups. This type of training is done in sets of 8 to 12 repetitions, using a weight just heavy enough so that only 12 repetitions can be produced.

Some suggested muscle-strength exercises are abdominal curls for a strong abdomen and lower back, and squats for strong shoulders, hips, lower buttocks, thighs, calves, and ankles. Lifting two 3-pound weights, which can be books, quart bottles filled with water, or standard weights purchased at a sporting goods store, is good for building strength in arm muscles. (There are ankle, body, and wrist weights also.) Take a day off in-between workouts to give muscles recovery and muscle-building time.

Muscle Endurance

Muscle-endurance exercises build stamina to help the body perform at its best. This training repeats the same exercise many times, using a relatively light weight. Vigorous exercises such as jogging, bicycling, and swimming are excellent for achieving muscle endurance. They also increase heart and lung efficiency and improve an athlete's overall personal appearance. Muscle-endurance training should only be done three times a week because muscle fibers tear slightly during exercise and need rest to rebuild themselves.

Cardiovascular Endurance

Cardiovascular endurance is achieved through exercises performed for at least 20 minutes. Walking, jogging, running, bicycling, swimming, dancing, and skipping rope are activities that raise the heart rate, take oxygen into the body, and move it to the muscles, which then provide the energy for the exercise that is being done.

Weather and unhealthful air sometimes interfere with outdoor endurance exercises, so gyms have become more and more popular with athletes. Stationary bicycles are widely available and can be "ridden" to fit a personal schedule that is not dependent on the weather. Other indoor endurance exercises include jogging in place, jumping jacks, and side hops. When exercising on a rug, wear gym socks; on a hard floor, shoes that cushion the feet are best.

Flexibility

There are numerous flexibility exercises—bends, stretches, swings, twists, lifts, and raisers—which stretch out muscles that have "tightened" from vigorous exercise. Muscle-pull injuries are common when flexibility is poor, even though muscle strength might be high. On the other hand, when flexibility is high but muscle strength low, dislocations can occur.

Conditioning Programs

Many athletes work on conditioning programs to build muscle strength and endurance, which can reduce the chance of an injury. They often play other sports to stay in shape and keep their stamina levels high in the off-season. Year-round conditioning is advocated by some coaches who prepare their athletes by dividing the year into phases or periods, with different goals and objectives for each period. Coaches at the highest levels of competition expect several hours per day of fitness training because they know that athletes who stay fit are less likely to sustain injuries and recover faster when they are injured.

Reconditioning

As important as conditioning programs are, a program of reconditioning is equally important after an athlete has suffered an injury. Athletes want to compete, but the decision to return to competition should be made by the player's parents, family physician, and coach, all working together.

A sprained ankle, for example, might be rehabilitated with easy jogging at first and then building up to running. Ice can be used to reduce any swelling that might occur, and/or an elastic bandage might be worn.

Everyone involved should be patient and not allow the athlete to return to play until the injury is no longer a problem. Semi-recovered cyclists can reinjure themselves and set back their recovery time.

Note: This book is in no way intended to be a substitute for the medical advice of a personal physician. We advise and encourage the reader to consult with his/her physician before beginning this or any other weight-management, exercise, or fitness program. The authors and the publisher disclaim any liability or loss, personal or otherwise, resulting from the suggestions in this book.

10

Safety and First Aid

Although bicycle riding is not considered a contact sport, an accident or injury can happen to anyone at any time. In cycling, the two most common mishaps are falls and collisions. Although most spills are not serious, you should never take a chance with an injured person. The following guidelines will help everyone optimally cope with an injured rider.

- **Remain Calm.** The injured cyclist's recovery may depend on the decisions you make, and it's hard to make accurate decisions when you're flustered. Moreover, your behavior may determine the reactions of others around you, including cyclists, parents, and spectators, and no one will benefit from extreme or hysterical reactions when level-headed judgment is called for.

- **Stay in Control.** Resist the urge to move an injured cyclist to a more comfortable location (such as under a shade tree). Only if the cyclist is in imminent danger should he or she be moved. Whenever there is any doubt as to the nature or extent of an injury, call for emergency assistance (fire, police, etc.). You may cover the injured person with a blanket or jacket to keep him warm and reduce the chance of shock, but let him stay where he is until help arrives.

- **Move Bicycle.** For safety reasons, it may be necessary in some cases to move fallen bicycles out of the path of oncoming traffic. Another option would be to flag oncoming traffic and route it around the accident site. In either case, be extremely careful—never put yourself or another person in danger by trying to salvage a fallen bike. Bicycles, no matter how fancy, can be replaced. Let the bike go; safety is your primary consideration.

The First Aid Kit

It is a good idea to keep a basic first aid kit on hand at all times. Many pharmacies and sporting goods stores carry well-stocked first aid kits, but if you want to put one together yourself, the following items should be included:

- Adhesive tape in different sizes
- Adhesive bandages of various sizes
- Antiseptic soap (for washing a wounded area)
- Antiseptic solution (for bug bites, minor scrapes)
- Aspirin, or its equivalent, for simple headaches (no medication should be given without written, parental permission, signed and dated, authorizing the disbursement of aspirin or any other medicine)
- Blanket to cover injured cyclist (warmth reduces chance of shock)
- Cold packs
- Elastic bandages (various sizes)
- Eyewash solution
- Gauze pads (various sizes)
- Hank's solution (trade name Save-a-Tooth®)
- Plastic bottle filled with fresh water

- Sterile cotton sheets (can be cut to fit)
- Scissors and perhaps an eyedropper
- Tissues and premoistened towelettes
- Tweezers (for splinters)
- Small utility knife; *e.g.,* a Swiss Army knife for use on trail rides

The phone number of the nearest ambulance service should be taped to the inside of the first aid kit. If you ride as a club or group, all cyclists should know where the first aid kit is stored, and where it will be kept at races and other events. The best first aid kit in the world does you no good if you can't find it when you need it. When riding at sanctioned events, make sure someone in your group knows the location of the closest telephone. Always keep some spare change in the kit so you won't have to hunt for coins in an emergency.

Treating Road Burns

Learning proper bike-handling skills will help reduce your chances of falling, but even the best cyclists fall occasionally. If you or someone in your cycling group falls, the following information will help you treat skin abrasions commonly known to cyclists as "road burns."

Road burns are graded by level of severity, similar to the grading system used for other types of burns: first, second, and third degree. First degree applies when there is only a reddening of skin. In a first-degree burn, the skin is not broken, and there is no bleeding. Generally, these are minor wounds and can be treated by washing the bruised area with clean, cool water and a mild antiseptic soap. If necessary, an ice bag may be applied for a few minutes to help reduce discomfort and take away any stinging sensation.

Second-degree burns are more serious. In this case, the injured person suffers reddening, broken skin, and bleeding. Frightening as it sounds—and, no doubt, looks at the time—most second-degree road burns heal beautifully and, believe it or not, rather quickly. Proper emergency treatment of the injured party promotes successful healing.

Keep the injured person quiet, preferably in a sitting or lying-down position. This helps to reduce the chance of shock and keeps an adequate supply of blood flowing to the brain. In cases of severe bleeding, your first concern should be to stanch the flow. Bind the wound and keep it bound. In any injury where there is excessive bleeding, do not worry about cleaning the wound. Your efforts should be directed toward stopping the bleeding and getting a doctor or rescue team to the injured person.

In cases of minor bleeding, you may attempt to clean the wound before bandaging it. Pour a bit of the antiseptic soap onto a wad of sterile cotton. Gently clean the wounded area of any surface debris, but leave deep probing to a qualified physician. To control bleeding and keep wounds clean, place a nonstick gauze pad over the abrasion. Cover that with a fresh cotton sheet; then bind the wound with an elastic wrap. Do not make your wrap too tight. For wounds covering a smaller area, repeat the cleaning procedure described above, but cover the wound with an adhesive bandage, cut to fit if necessary.

If the injured person remains conscious, give him fresh, cool water to drink. Fresh water flowing through the system helps the lymph glands carry away any infectious bacteria. If the injured person is unconscious or drifts in and out of consciousness, refrain from giving him anything to eat or drink. He could easily choke, causing even more serious problems.

The injured person should be taken to a doctor for follow-up treatment as soon as possible. Extensive cleaning or suturing should be attempted only by a qualified physician. Once a second-degree wound begins to heal, the fresh, tender skin must be protected from the sun. Young skin does not have the protective capabilities of older skin and must be shielded from harmful ultraviolet rays.

Third-degree road burns are the most serious. In this type of burn, the skin has been entirely removed, possibly exposing underlying layers of muscle and/or bone. An injury of this type demands urgent professional care. Do not move the injured person. Summon a doctor or rescue team him immediately. Fortunately, most cycling falls are not this severe. We mention such serious accidents here only so you will have an idea of the degrees of injury possible, and an understanding of how best to handle each situation. Stay calm, think, and do the best you can under the circumstances. When in the slightest doubt, call for emergency assistance. This is the smartest call you can possibly make.

Handling a Dislodged Tooth

Most times when a tooth has been knocked out it can be replanted and retained for life, especially if the tooth has been properly handled. One critical factor determining a successful replant is the care and handling of a dislodged tooth.

The best way to store a tooth is to immerse it in a pH-balanced, buffered, cell-preserving solution, such as Hank's or Viaspan® (used for transplant organ storage). Hank's solution (under the trade name Save-a-Tooth®) may be purchased over-the-counter at many drug stores. It will store the tooth in a safe container for 24 hours and has a shelf life of two years. With the use of a proper storage and transport container, there is an excellent chance of having a dislodged tooth successfully replanted.

Vision and Corrective Lenses

Your vision, just like the strength in your arms and legs, is an important part of your overall performance. The demands on your visual system during sporting activities are rigorous. To ride your best, you must know what is behind you, beside you, and in front of you at all times, and this takes a variety of vision skills. If your natural vision affects your athletic performance, ask your doctor about glasses or contact lenses.

Today's eye-care specialists use a wide variety of lens materials. One very positive development is the availability of new impact-resistant lenses for use in prescription glasses. These lenses are attractive, affordable, and lightweight, and will not shatter if broken.

Another option is contact lenses. Available in hard and soft lens materials, contacts offer many excellent advantages to the athlete. For best results, tell your doctor about the type of cycling that you do. That information will be helpful to the doctor in selecting the best lenses for you. If you wear contact lenses, take your cleaning and wetting solutions with you to all cycling events, and notify your coach that you are wearing contacts.

Getting a foreign object in the eye is the most common eye problem associated with cycling. Fortunately, such foreign objects are usually in the form of minor irritants, such as dust, dirt, or sand. Goggles will help protect your eyes, especially on windy days. Your local bicycle shop will have many styles to choose from—select one that fits securely and allows a wide field of vision.

Care of the Eyes

More serious injuries, such as a blow to the head, may produce bleeding in or under the skin near the eye, causing a "black eye." An ice pack will reduce swelling until a doctor can evaluate the injury.

Fortunately, the eye has a number of natural defenses. It is recessed in a bony socket, and the quick-blinking reflexes of the eyelids and eyelashes deflect most foreign particles. Also, natural tears wash away most minor irritants. If you *do* get something in your eye, follow these simple guidelines:

- Do not rub your eye or use a dirty cloth or finger to remove the obstruction.

- Irritants can often be eliminated by looking down and pulling the eyelid forward and down. Make sure your hands are clean.

- If you see a particle floating on your eye, gently remove it with a clean, sterile cloth or apply an eyewash to flush the obstruction.

Whatever you do for recreation, your vision plays a vital role in helping you enjoy the sport and perform at your best. Your eyes deserve the best of care.

Wrist and Hand Injuries

Injuries to the wrists and hands are most often related to falling, although fingers can be "jammed" during a collision. To reduce the possibility of wrist and hand injuries, follow these simple guidelines:

- Prior to riding, remove all cosmetic jewelry. If you wear a medical-alert bracelet, continue to wear it while cycling, but make sure it is snug enough not to catch on handlebars or brake and shift levers.

- Avoid riding with your fingers straight out. Keep your fingertips and knuckles curled back toward your palms, and keep your thumbs resting alongside your index fingers.

- Avoid putting a "death grip" on your handlebars. Hold your bike firmly, but allow some flex into your elbows and shoulders. This will help prevent stress and muscle fatigue from settling in your hands, thereby reducing your chances of wrist and hand injuries.

- Gloves are a good way to protect your hands. If you fall, gloves keep your hands from getting scratched; while you ride, gloves protect your hands from friction on the handlebars and from the elements, especially the sun.

Transporting Tips

To be on the safe side, cyclists who have suffered an upper extremity injury should be evaluated by a doctor. To safely transport a person with an arm, wrist, or hand injury, follow these steps:

- A finger with mild swelling can be gently taped to an adjacent finger.

- An elastic bandage may be gently wrapped around an injured wrist to give the wrist support. Do not wrap heavily and do not pull the bandage tightly.

- If possible, place a pillow in the rider's lap and allow him or her to rest the injured hand on the pillow. Do not bunch the pillow around the injury.

Naturally, if the injury is severe and there is an obvious deformity, seek professional help as soon as possible. If the cyclist has a possible broken leg or arm, the best approach is not to move the leg or arm in any manner. A cold pack can be used to lessen discomfort until medical personnel arrive, and the cyclist should be kept warm with a blanket or covering to avoid shock. Fractures and broken bones are the same whether the bone is cracked, chipped, or broken. A fracture can be recognized by some or all of the following conditions:

- A part of the body is bent or twisted from its normal shape

- A bone has pierced the skin

- Swelling is severe and more than the swelling associated with a typical sprain or bruise

- Hand or foot becomes extremely cold, which may indicate pinching of a major blood vessel

Youngsters heal faster than adults, so it's important to get them prompt medical attention when a fracture occurs.

Ice and Heat Treatments

If a cyclist is injured, elevate the injury (if possible) and apply an ice pack. Use ice instead of heat because cold reduces both swelling and pain. Leave the ice pack on until it becomes uncomfortable. Allow the injured person to rest for 15 minutes, then reapply the ice pack. Repeat this procedure until any swelling abates or, in more serious cases, until professional medical help arrives.

RICE (rest, ice, compression, and elevation) is the recommended way to manage an injury and is about all you should do in the way of self–treatment. Have the cyclist stop and rest, apply ice, compress with an elastic bandage, and elevate the injured arm, leg, knee, or ankle. RICE reduces the swelling of most cycling injuries and speeds recovery. Over the next few days, the injury should be treated with two to three 20-minute sessions per day at two and one-half hour intervals. This should provide noticeable improvement. Don't overdo the icing; 20 minutes is long enough. In most cases, after two or three days, or when the swelling has stopped, heat can be applied in the form of warm-water soaks. Fifteen minutes of warm soaking, along with a gradual return to motion, will speed the healing process right along. Specially shaped pads are useful for knee and ankle injuries, and they can be used in combination with ice, compression, and elevation.

Another approach to use after two or three days, and if your doctor agrees, is to begin motion, strength, and alternative (MSA) exercise. The American Institute for Preventive Medicine recommends:

- Motion: Moving the injured area and reestablishing its range of motion.

- Strength: Working to increase the strength of the injured area once any inflammation subsides and your range of motion starts to return.

- Alternative: Regularly doing an alternative exercise that does not stress the injury.

Seek the advice of a sports-medicine professional prior to starting your own treatment plan.

Guidelines for Reducing Injuries

Although no amount of planning and preparation can guarantee that a cyclist will never fall or be injured, there are many things that can be done to reduce the possibility of injury.

Inspect your bike and equipment daily. If you spot a developing problem, take care of it immediately. Do not ride with faulty equipment, no matter how minor the problem may seem. Get it fixed.

Avoid riding alone, especially on unknown or hazardous trails. Always tell a reliable person where you are going and what time to expect you back. Then keep to that schedule. Ride with a buddy whenever possible.

Novices of any age should avoid riding after dark. Experienced riders should wear reflective clothing and attach reflective pads to their helmets and shoes. Keep headlamp and reflectors clean and in good repair. Most nighttime collisions are the direct result of drivers not being able to see the rider.

Even during the day it is beneficial to wear clothing that allows drivers to see you, as far ahead as possible. Bright fluorescent colors work best.

Always wear a safety helmet and proper footwear. There are many good cycling shoes to choose from, but even a good sturdy pair of sneakers is better than going barefoot.

If you like to ride on a motocross-type course, check the course for hazards *before* you ride. Debris should always be cleared away, and dangerous obstacles, such as large boulders, should be removed or at least flagged.

Take water with you on the trail, and always have a supply of fresh water at every cycling event.

Warm up and stretch before you ride. If the weather is breezy or cold, keep your body covered and avoid drafts. A proper warm-up routine will reduce the possibility of a pulled muscle or other injury. When you return from riding, get out of your cycling clothes as soon as possible. Damp, sweaty clothes increase the chance of muscle stiffness and skin irritation. Shower and dress warmly as quickly as you can.

Always seek prompt medical attention for an injured person. If you do not know what to do, call for emergency assistance. Do not move an injured cyclist unless he or she is in immediate danger at that location. If you will have to wait long for assistance, cover the injured person with a lightweight blanket. Warmth reduces the chance of shock.

11

Bicycle Maintenance

No matter what type of bicycle you have, you need to take proper care of it. There are many simple maintenance tasks you can perform yourself to prolong both the life and appearance of your bike.

Cleaning

Check your bike after every ride. If you are lucky enough to have a hanging rack, lift your bike onto the rack before you begin the cleaning process. If you do not have a hanging rack, simply park your bike in a clean, dust-free area before you begin cleaning up. Finding a clean environment is important because dust and sand can blow onto the freshly-oiled parts of your bike, creating a sticky mess.

If the bike has gotten very muddy, you may wish to squirt it off with a hose before beginning your cleaning routine. Do not drown the bike. Just get the mud off; then bring the bike into the garage or work shed for a thorough cleaning.

Dip a sponge into a bucket of warm, soapy water and give the bike a good wiping down. Use a mild laundry soap or car washing soap; never use anything abrasive. Don't forget to clean those hard-to-reach places. For those particularly difficult areas, you can also use any of several commercial degreasers.

Once you have given your bike a good washing, go over it lightly with a clean, damp sponge to pick up all traces of soap. Immediately go over the entire bike with a dry Turkish or terry-cloth towel. Do not let water dry on the bike itself. You will probably need more than one towel to do the job right. If one towel gets wet, use another. The important thing is to wipe the bike dry.

An old toothbrush works very well for cleaning the chain. Check the chain for wear and adjustment. If it needs to be tightened, do so. Riding with a floppy chain not only is dangerous, but also puts wear and tear on other moving parts. Keep the chain clean and the tension properly adjusted.

Once the bike is clean, it is time to oil and grease moving parts. Use bicycle oil, not household oil. You can get bicycle oil at your local bike shop. The chain, gears, and brake calipers all need oil. Tire hubs, nuts, and bolts need clean, dust-free bearing grease. If you only have oil, use it. The important thing is to keep moving parts lubricated.

Use a stiff brush to remove tiny stones and pieces of glass from front and rear tires. Check them carefully for foreign particles and listen for slow air leaks. If you hear a leak, repair the tire before riding again. Use a tire gauge to determine tire pressure. If pressure in one or both tires is low, inflate each tire to the recommended pressure before riding again. Maintaining proper tire pressure will help prolong the life of your tires and make your rides smoother and more enjoyable.

Give the bike a final inspection. Check brake cables for proper tension. Check handlebar grips for cracks, tears, or debris. If the damage is extensive, replace them before you injure your hands. Check your bike seat for wear and tear, and if the damage is extensive, replace your bike seat, too. You do not want to be out on a long ride and have your seat start giving you trouble.

Storage

Cleaning is important, but so is storage. Here are some tips to make bicycle storage safer and more convenient.

• Keep your bike protected from the weather, especially rain and hot sun. The damage from rain is obvious, but did you know that direct sunlight is just as damaging? Sun rots your tires and cables and dries out areas that should be kept lubricated.

• Store your bike in an area where it won't be in anyone's way. It's not fair that passersby should have to dodge your bike to get through a doorway. Be polite and keep your bike out of aisles and off sidewalks and paths. Also, if your bike is out of the way, it's less likely to be knocked over.

• Keep your bike locked and tethered to a strong, immovable post.

• Finally, if you are not going to ride your bike for more than a month, devise some way to hang it by its frame. It's not good for the tires to have to support all of the bike's weight on one small area.

The longer you have your bike, the more you will get to know it. You will be able to feel when something is not right. Knowing your bicycle well means you will know to take it to a reputable bike shop before major damage can occur. Read as much as you can about bicycle repair and ask questions of experts. The more you know about your bicycle, the better you will be at repairing and maintaining it yourself.

12

Glossary

Aerobic A physical condition in which all the body parts are working to maximum effectiveness.

Attack An aggressive, high-speed move away from other riders.

Backstraight The part of the track farthest from the grandstand.

Blocking Legally impeding the progress of riders in the pack to allow teammates a better chance for success.

Breakaway A rider or group of riders who have outrun the pack.

Bridge To escape one group of riders and join another group farther ahead.

Butted Tube A type of tubing found in expensive bike frames. The metal is very thin throughout except at each end, where it thickens to provide strength at tube intersections.

Calipers Bicycle brakes actuated by hand levers.

Categories The division of USA Cycling classes into smaller groups, based on riding ability and experience.

Century A 100-mile race.

Chase Riding to catch a breakaway.

Circuit A multi-lap event on a course that usually is 2 miles or more in length.

Cleat A metal or plastic fitting on the sole of a cycling shoe.

Clinchers Conventional tire with a separate inner tube.

Club Ride A training ride among members of bicycle clubs.

Criterium A mass-start race covering numerous laps of a course that is usually 1 mile or less in length.

Dab Touching the ground with a foot or hand. Adds one point to the rider's score.

Derailleur The mechanism that moves the chain from gear to gear.

Disqualification A penalty that results in a rider, or a team, losing its place in a race. A disqualified rider or team becomes ineligible for the rest of the race.

Downstroke The time when a rider's foot is pushing down on a pedal; the moment the greatest amount of energy is displaced to the pedal.

Drafting Riding in the *slipstream* (see below) of the rider ahead. Drafting cuts wind resistance and saves a great deal of energy.

Dropped Out A rider who has fallen behind his group.

Echelon When a crosswind is blowing, each rider positions himself to the side of and slightly behind the rider immediately in front. If the wind is coming from the right, the line of riders will angle off to the left side of the person in front, thereby lessening the negative effect of the wind.

Fat Tire A common term for the mountain bike and everything that has to do with it.

Feed Zone A designated area along a racecourse where support crews may hand food and drink to racers.

Field The main group of riders. Also known as the "pack," "bunch," or "peloton."

Field Sprint A dash to the finish line by the largest group of riders remaining in a race; usually, but not always, a pack toward the front.

Forcing the Pace To increase the pace of a ride to the point that other riders have trouble maintaining the speed and begin to flounder. This tactic works well in racing, but should be avoided on pleasure rides.

Gap The distance between the leaders and the field, measured in time.

Gnarly A mountain bike term that denotes admiration and toughness when applied to a person; when applied to a terrain, a way to say "scary" without sounding scared.

Granny Gear The lowest gear on a mountain bike.

Hammering Riding hard; going all out.

Hanging On Barely maintaining contact at the back of the pack.

Homestraight The part of the track from the last turn to the finish line.

Hook An accident in which two riders collide by locking handlebars or wheels together. To avoid a hook, pleasure riders should allow at least a full arm's length side-to-side and a bicycle length front-to-back.

Hover In mountain biking, to adjust your weight by lifting your rear end out of the saddle. Relieves your weight only long enough to go over a bump.

International Suspension A penalty that causes the loss of participation in either international events or USA Cycling events.

Invitational Race A race with riders who have been invited to participate by the organizer of the race.

Jerk Mountain bike word for any rider in the vicinity of an accident.

Jump Any quick, aggressive acceleration; a move frequently used when making an *attack* (see above).

Keirin A sprint featuring six cyclists drafting behind a motorcycle.

LAB League of American Bicyclists. Founded in 1880 as the League of American Wheelmen, this is the oldest organized body of cyclists in the United States. Among other activities, this politically active group initiates and supports legislation beneficial to cyclists.

Lead Out   A race tactic in which a rider accelerates to his maximum speed for the benefit of a teammate behind him. The second rider then leaves the *slipstream* (see below) and sprints past the leader at even greater speed. This move is usually executed near the finish line.

LSD   Long, steady distance. A training technique that calls for continuous rides of at least two hours, done entirely at an aerobic pace.

Lugs   Metal fittings at the intersections of tubes in a frame.

Madison   A pairs track race in which teammates relay one another into contention.

Mass Start   Events in which all contestants leave the starting line at the same time.

Minuteman   In a *time trial* (see below), the minuteman is the rider who leaves the starting line one place in front of you. So named because in most time trials, riders leave at one-minute intervals.

Mishap   A crash or a mechanical accident, *e.g.*, a tire puncture or a critical component failure. Mis-assembly, insufficient tightening of a part, or inadequate gluing are not mishaps.

Mixed Team   A race where one-half of the riders are women.

Mixte   A frame design that has two straight tubes

going from the head tube to the rear stay ends, both being attached to the seat tube. This configuration produces a stronger frame than the traditional dropped- or scooped-frame construction.

MSA Acronym for motion, strength, alternative. An approach to managing an injury. *See also* RICE.

Pace Line A single-file formation in which each rider takes a turn at the front, breaking the wind for the group before pulling off and dropping to the rear of the pack.

Panniers Large saddlebags used by touring and recreational riders. These come in pairs and are mounted on a rack that allows them to hang along each side of the rear wheel. Panniers over the front wheel are seen less frequently.

Potato Chip A wrenched wheel on a mountain bike.

Power Train The components directly involved with making the rear wheel turn.

Prime Pronounced *preem*, this is a sprint within a race. Riders who successfully execute this move can earn extra points or prizes.

PSI Pounds per square inch.

Pull To ride at the front of a pack.

Pull Off To move to the side after leading so that another rider can come to the front.

Race Entry   The process of paying the fee and committing to participate.

Race Meet   One or more races that may take place over one or more days. Requires a single race permit.

Race Registration   The time when riders present their licenses and obtain their numbers and related race information.

Racing Age   Your age on December 31 of the current year.

RICE   An acronym for rest, ice, compression, and elevation. The formula for immediate management of an injury. *See also* MSA.

Road Race   A mass-start race that goes from one point to another point, covers one large loop, or is held on a circuit longer than that used for a criterium (see below).

Saddle   A bicycle seat.

Saddle Sores   Chafing between the legs. These abrasions must be tended to right away or they can lead to serious problems.

SAG Wagon   A support vehicle that follows a group of riders. Its purpose is to carry equipment and lend assistance where needed.

Session   Races with no major time breaks. Usually the procedure for championships.

Single Track   Path or trail only wide enough for one mountain bike rider at a time.

Sit on a Wheel   To ride directly behind someone, thereby receiving benefit of the *draft* or slipstream (see below).

Slingshot A move to sprint around another rider at top speed after drafting.

Slipstream The area of low air resistance behind a moving cyclist.

Snakebite In a tire, a double puncture that looks like two fang holes. This is the most common flat tire encountered by mountain bikers.

Soft Pedal To rotate the pedals without actually applying power.

Sprint A short acceleration to maximum speed.

Sprinter A rider who excels in short power bursts.

Stage Race A multi-day event consisting of point-to-point and circuit road races, time trials, and criteriums (see above). The winner is the rider with the lowest elapsed time for all stages.

Team Time Trial A race against the clock with two or more riders forming a team and working together.

Throw the Bike A racing technique in which a rider pushes the bike as far ahead of his or her body as possible without losing control, thereby hoping to cross the finish line ahead of a competitor.

Time Trial A race against the clock in which individual riders start at set intervals and cannot give aid or receive it from others on the course.

Trackstand Balancing in place on the track or at a stoplight.

Tubular A lightweight racing tire that has the tube permanently sewn inside the casing. The tire is glued onto the rim.

Turnaround The point where cyclists reverse direction on an out-and-back time-trial course.

Upstroke When a rider is pulling up on a pedal.

USA Cycling The organization in charge of cycling in America. It makes the rules, sanctions the events, and licenses the competitors.

Velodrome An indoor or outdoor track for bicycle racing with banked turns and flat straightaways. Usually made of wood (indoors) or concrete (outdoors).

Wheels Your bike.

Windup Steady acceleration designed to peak with an all-out effort.

Youth Race A race on a closed course for riders who are below 10 years old. Riders up to 15 years old may participate if there is no junior race for them.

13

Olympic and Cycling Organizations

The organization of, and participation in, the Olympic Games requires the cooperation of a number of independent organizations.

The International Olympic Committee (IOC)

The IOC is responsible for determining where the Games will be held. It is also the obligation of its membership to uphold the principles of the Olympic Ideal and Philosophy beyond any personal, religious, national, or political interest. The IOC is responsible for sustaining the Olympic Movement.

The members of the IOC are individuals who act as the IOC's representatives in their respective countries, not as delegates of their countries within the IOC. The members meet once a year at the IOC Session. They retire at the end of the calendar year in which they turn 70 years old, unless they were elected before the opening of the 110th Session (December 11, 1999). In that case, they must retire at the age of 80. Members elected before 1966 are members for life. The IOC chooses and elects its members from among such persons as its nominations committee considers qualified. There are currently 113 members and 19 honorary members.

The International Olympic Committee's address is—

Chateau de Vidy, CH-1007
Lausanne, Switzerland
Tel: (41-21) 621-6111   Fax: (41-21) 621-6216
www.olympic.org

The National Olympic Committees

Olympic Committees have been created, with the design and objectives of the IOC, to prepare national teams to participate in the Olympic Games. Among the tasks of these committees is to promote the Olympic Movement and its principles at the national level.

The national committees work closely with the IOC in all aspects related to the Games. They are also responsible for applying the rules concerning eligibility of athletes for the Games. Today there are more than 150 national committees throughout the world.

The U.S. Olympic Committee's address is—

Olympic House
One Olympic Plaza
Colorado Springs, CO 80909-5760
Tel: (719) 632-5551   Fax: (719) 578-6216
www.olympic-usa.org

Cycling Associations/Collegiate Cycling

USA Cycling
One Olympic Plaza
Colorado Springs, CO 80909
Tel: (719) 578-4581   FAX: (719) 578-4628
www.usacycling.org

International Cycling Union
Union Cycliste Internationale
37 Route de Chavannes
Case Postale CH 1000 Lausanne 23 Suisse
Tel:+41 21 622 0580   FAX: +41 21 622 0588
www.uci.ch

International Mountain Bicycling Association (IMBA)
1121 Broadway Ste 203
P.O. Box 7578
Boulder, CO 80306
Tel: (888) 442-4622   FAX: (303) 545-9026
www.imba.com

League of American Bicyclists (LAB)
1612 K Street, NW, Suite #401
Washington, DC 20006
Tel: (202) 822-1333   FAX: (202) 822-1334

National Collegiate Cycling Association (NCCA)
NCCA National Headquarters
One Olympic Plaza
Colorado Springs, CO 80909
Tel: (719) 578-4581   FAX: (719) 578-4628
www.usacycling.org

National Off-Road Bicycle Association (NORBA)
NORBA National Headquarters
One Olympic Plaza
Colorado Springs, CO 80909
Tel: (719) 578-4717   FAX: (719) 578-4628
www.usacycling.org

Tandem Club of America (TCA)
306 West Union Street
 Morganton, NC 28655-3729
Tel: 704-437-1068
www.mindspring.com/~strauss/tca.html

Ultra-Marathon Cycling Association (UMCA)
PO Box 18028
Boulder, CO 80308-1028
Tel: (303) 545-9566   FAX: (303) 545-9619
www.ultracycling.com   e-mail UMCAHQ@aol.com

14

2000 Olympic Games

Eighteen medal events were held at the Sydney Olympics: twelve in track cycling, four in road racing, and two in mountain biking. In the overall standings, Germany led the pack with ten medals, followed by France with eight. Leontien Zijlaard of the Netherlands was a standout individual performer, winning three gold medals.

Marty Nothstein brought home the gold for the United States in the men's sprint, while Lance Armstrong had to settle for bronze in the men's individual time trial. Among the women, Mari Holden captured a silver in the individual time trial, but Chris Witty failed in her attempt to become the first American woman to win medals at both the Olympic Summer and Winter Games.

Track Races

Men's 1km Time Trial

Jason Queally of Great Britain, Stefan Nimke of Germany, and Shane Kelly of Australia finished one, two, and three, with times of 1:01.609 (an Olympic record), 1:02.487, and 1:02.818, respectively. U.S. cyclist Jonas Carney was 14th with a time of 1:05.968.

Women's 500m Time Trial

This trial was won by Felicia Ballanger of France, followed by Michelle Ferris of Australia and Jiang Cuihua of China, with times of 34.140, 34.696 and 34.768, respectively. Off the pace was U.S. competitor Chris Witty, who finished fifth at 35.230. Witty, who won silver and bronze medals in speedskating at the 1998 Olympic Winter Games, did not compete in any other cycling events at Sydney.

Men's Individual Pursuit

The U.S. failed to qualify in the preliminaries for this race. Two riders from Germany, Robert Bartko and Jens Lehmann, took the gold and silver medals, while Brad McGee of Australia won the bronze.

Men's Olympic Sprint

In this team event making its debut at the 2000 Games, France won the gold medal. Great Britain and Australia captured the silver and bronze medals, respectively.

Men's Team Pursuit

New world marks were set twice in little more than one hour during this 4,000-meter event, as the 4:00.830 record set by Ukraine was broken by the German entrants with a time of 3:59.710. Ukraine claimed the silver medal, with the bronze going to Great Britain.

Women's Individual Pursuit

The gold medal in this 3,000-meter event was claimed by the Netherlands, followed by France and Great Britain. All three winners overcame medical disabilities on their way to these

Games. Leontien Zijlaard of the Netherlands battled an eating disorder in the 1990s but by 1998 had come back to win gold and silver medals at the World Road Championships. Marion Clignet of France has epilepsy and arthritis, while Yvonne McGregor of Great Britain has suffered from back problems.

Men's Sprint

U.S. national champion Marty Nothstein, a silver medalist at Atlanta in 1996, took the gold in Sydney this time around, finishing ahead of Florian Rousseau of France and two-time Olympic gold medalist Jens Fiedler of Germany. It was the first gold in cycling for the U.S. since 1984 in Los Angeles.

Men's Keirin

Run for the first time at the Olympic Summer Games, the men's Keirin track race was won by Florian Rousseau of France. Gary Neiwand of Australia won the silver medal, and Jens Fiedler of Germany took the bronze. Marty Nothstein's effort for the U.S. was blocked successfully—not an illegal tactic in Keirin racing—and he finished fifth.

Men's Madison

This race was won by Scott McGrory and Brett Aitken of Australia, Etienne de Wilde and Matthew Gilmore of Belgium, and Marco Villa and Silvio Martinello of Italy, in that order. Australia's gold medal was its first in cycling since Los Angeles in 1984.

Women's Sprint

No American women medaled in this event, which was won by Felicia Ballanger of France. Oxana Grichina of Russia won the silver, and Iryna Yanovych of Ukraine captured the bronze.

Women's Points Race

The gold medal was won by Antonella Bellutti of Italy. Leontien Zijlaard of the Netherlands took her second medal, the silver, and Olga Slioussareva of Russia won the bronze.

Men's Points Race

The medals went to Juan Llaneras of Spain, Milton Wynants of Uruguay, and Alexey Markov of Russia, in that order.

Road Races
Women's Road Race

Claiming her third medal and second gold, Leontien Zijlaard of the Netherlands completed the race with a time of 3:06:31.001. Hanka Kupfernagel of Germany was the silver medalist with a time of 3:06:31.002, followed by Diana Ziliute of Lithuania for the bronze in 3:06:31.003.

Men's Road Race

This grueling 239.4-kilometer race was won by Germany's Jan Ullrich with a time of 5:29:08. Ullrich, ranked No. 1 in the world in road racing, was followed by Alexandre Vinokourov of Kazakhstan with a time of 5:29:17 for the silver, and Germany's Andreas Kloeden with a time of 5:29:20 for the bronze. Americans George Hincapie (5:30:34) and Lance Armstrong (5:30:37) finished eighth and thirteenth, respectively.

Men's Individual Time Trial

On a windy course extending 46.8 kilometers, Viacheslav Ekimov of Russia won the men's individual time trial in 57:40. Germany's

Jan Ullrich was the silver medal winner with a time of 57:48, just eight seconds back. American Lance Armstrong—a hero to cyclists and fans around the world, both for his Tour de France victories and for his remarkable recovery from cancer—finished with the bronze medal in 58:14.

Women's Individual Time Trial

Leontien Zijlaard of the Netherlands won her third gold medal (and fourth overall) of these Games with a time of 42 minutes on the 28.97-kilometer course. Close behind was American Mari Holden for the silver with a time of 42:37. The bronze went to Jeannie Longo-Ciprelli of France with a time of 42:52.

Mountain Bike Races

Women's Cross-Country

Paola Pezzo of Italy took the gold with a time of 1:49:24. Barbara Blatter of Switzerland (1:49:51) won the silver, and Margarita Fullana of Spain (1:49:57) the bronze. Cyclists from Russia, Canada, and Australia followed, with Alison Dunlap of the U.S. finishing seventh in 1:53:53.

Men's Cross-Country

Miguel Martinez of France won the gold with a time of 2:09:02, followed by Filip Meirhaeghe of Belgium (2:10:05) for the silver and Christoph Sauser of Switzerland (2:11:21) for the bronze.